"How long will it take me to work off my debt?"

"Is that a yes?"

"No, it's a question," Tanna replied. "How long?"

"I need someone here full-time for another two weeks, part-time for at least four weeks after that."

"Your sisters and mom aren't prepared to help you?" Tanna asked, looking for an escape.

"Of course they are, but I like them. I don't see why they should have to put up with my foul mood when you can."

"Because I owe you," Tanna said, sounding miserable.

Yep, she did. And also because he couldn't imagine her walking out of his life again. Not until, he assured himself, he knew every inch of that luscious body.

* * *

Second Chance Temptation is part of the Love in Boston series.

Dear Reader,

Here is Levi Brogan's story, the fifth book in my Love in Boston series.

At nineteen, Tanna is gravely injured in a car accident. After spending months in the hospital, she becomes engaged to Levi Brogan, who witnessed her accident. But Tanna has many doubts about marrying Levi—or anyone at all—and she leaves Boston, and Levi, a few days before their wedding.

Ten years pass and quick affairs are now Levi's style. He was badly hurt by Tanna and has no plans to put his heart on the line again.

Tanna, now a highly qualified EMT, is suffering from PTSD. Suspended from her job, she decides to return to Boston to confront her past. She visits Levi to apologize and finds out that he has injured his knee and shoulder after falling off his dirt bike. Tanna tries to apologize, but Levi isn't interested in apologies. The only thing he needs is a nurse and a little revenge.

But Levi finds himself more intrigued by this woman than ever before, and soon Tanna realizes that leaving Boston again will be harder than ever...

But she must...mustn't she?

Happy reading,

Joss

Connect with me at www.josswoodbooks.com

Twitter: @josswoodbooks

Facebook: Joss Wood Author

JOSS WOOD

SECOND CHANCE TEMPTATION

HARLEQUIN®DESIRE

Recycling programs
for this product may
not exist in your area.

ISBN-13: 978-1-335-60401-9

Second Chance Temptation

Printed in U.S.A.

Joss Wood loves books and traveling—especially to the wild places of Southern Africa and, well, anywhere. She's a wife, a mom to two teenagers and slave to two cats. After a career in local economic development, she now writes full-time. Joss is a member of Romance Writers of America and Romance Writers of South Africa.

Books by Joss Wood

Harlequin Desire

Love in Boston

Friendship on Fire
Hot Christmas Kisses
The Rival's Heir
Second Chance Temptation

Dynasties: Secrets of the A-list

Redeemed by Passion

Visit her Author Profile page at Harlequin.com, or josswoodbooks.com, for more titles.

You can find Joss Wood on Facebook, along with other Harlequin Desire authors, at Facebook.com/harlequindesireauthors!

One

Levi Brogan hurt.

Everywhere.

That's what happened when you leave your dirt bike for a make-out session with a gravel road lined with rocks.

His ass was now welded to a chair, partially because his leg was in plaster from above his knee down to his ankle, but mostly because moving anything more than his eyelids hurt. He'd not only broken his patella but also managed to pull a muscle in his left rotator cuff, so using crutches was like stabbing himself repeatedly in the shoulder.

Wah-wah-wah…

God, he was so over himself and his injuries, but

he was rapidly coming to the conclusion he could do with some help.

Someone who wasn't his mother or his sister. He loved them but, God, they never shut up. Ever. And if they weren't talking about wedding guests or honeymoons or babies or flowers, they were fussing over him.

By the time he'd kicked them out earlier this morning, he was close to overdosing on estrogen. Levi now deeply regretted his show of independence and there was a good chance that, by nightfall, he might swallow his pride and send out an SOS.

Levi pushed his hand through his hair, feeling utterly frustrated. His world was now confined to the bottom level of his home. Working out in his state-of-the-art gym in the basement was, obviously, not possible. He wasn't able to climb the stairs leading to his master bedroom, so he was sleeping on the sofa in the media room and using the downstairs bathroom to clean up. He would kill for a hot shower, but he needed help to get in and out of the bathtub. And right now, the kitchen was a million miles away.

And he was hungry.

Levi looked at his crutches, not sure if he had the energy to make the trek to find food, and checked the pain level in his shoulder. It was still screaming from walking the ten yards to the bathroom. Food was, unless he took another painkiller, out of the question. And every time he took a painkiller without food, he tossed his cookies.

Rock, let me introduce you to hard place.

Levi heard a knock on his front door and frowned. His family used the back door leading into the kitchen. And they all announced their presence. The extended Brogan family was not a quiet bunch. The Murphy guys were also frequent visitors and they also used the back door, knowing it was rarely locked. Business associates who needed to see him would've called to make an appointment and the rest of his small circle of friends were at work. And if they had a day off, they would've given him a heads-up via a text message.

End result: Levi had no idea who was knocking on his front door. A reporter? A photographer? The press had ambushed him when he left the hospital, the camera flashes making his headache a hundred times worse. He hadn't responded to any of their nearly indecipherable questions, and neither had his mom or his sisters. His dad had loved the press, but Levi and his mom and siblings didn't.

Despite the Brogans shunning the limelight, the tabloid press paid him, and his sisters, far too much attention, all because they were the children of Boston's most successful businessman and bon vivant, Ray Brogan. And, because those bottom-feeders loved drama, there had been a few articles about Levi's accident, reminding the residents of Boston that he and his father had had a volatile relationship. The press took great delight in telling the world he'd spurned Ray's offer to take over Brogan LLC , a holding company that owned and operated companies in many different sectors and that Levi, reserved, private and taciturn, wasn't the man his father was.

He wasn't as charming, as exciting, as loud or as volatile. Thank God.

Levi didn't make rash decisions, never made promises he couldn't keep, didn't take huge risks, causing the people he loved anxiety. Ray got off on risk and adrenaline—betting every cent on huge deals that might or might not come off. He made impulsive decisions—buying companies without doing due diligence—and calling people who suggested caution—mainly Levi—unimaginative and boring.

Ray's successes had been stratospheric, his failures equally impressive. Levi's mom had ridden the roller coaster; Levi, on joining the family firm after college, couldn't handle his father's volatility and resigned after a year.

His father called him dull and a coward, not cut out for a high-stakes world. Levi had never understood his father, who never felt embarrassed or chastised. He just blustered and BS'd his way through the criticism, and the world seemed to love him even more for his confidence, his brashness.

Levi was the exact opposite; he was not, and never would be, a fan of failure, not privately or publicly. He preferred to be the master of his own ship, avoiding storms rather than sailing directly into them. He liked to be in control. But the world expected him to be like his famous father, so whenever he showed even a hint of his father's impulsive nature—and apparently crashing his dirt bike qualified—he made the news.

Levi used his crutch to lift the drape covering the window of his study, through which he could see the road and his driveway. An unfamiliar SUV sat in his driveway, too expensive to belong to an intrepid reporter.

He hoped.

The knock came again and Levi bellowed a quick "Come in!" But, honestly, if he could persuade his visitor to make him a sandwich and a hot cup of coffee, he'd listen to a pitch for an interview, or from a salesman.

He was that desperate.

"I'm in the media room. Down the hallway, second door on your left."

Levi heard the front door closing and, judging by the hesitant steps, knew his visitor wasn't someone who had constant access to his house.

"For God's sake," Levi muttered, impatient. "Second door on the left."

"I heard you. I'm not deaf."

The words hit his ears at the same time she appeared in his doorway, and Levi stared at her, not sure whether his incredibly strong pain pills were causing hallucinations.

Black jeans and a thin, mint-colored sweater hugged her curves under a thigh-length leather jacket. A multi-colored scarf held back curls and her face was thinner, older and, God, so beautiful. Levi gripped the arm of his chair, physically grounding himself, fighting the instinct to rush her, to pull her into his arms and bury his face in her neck, in her lustrous hair. He needed to inhale the scent of her skin, to know whether it was as soft and creamy as it looked.

He wanted to strip her naked, to finally feel her round breast in his hand, to find out whether her nipples were as luscious as he imagined, her core as warm, as spicy, as the rest of her.

So much time had passed and Levi felt shocked at how much he wanted her. Unable to stop himself, he drank her in. Those light green eyes fringed with long, thick black lashes fascinated him and he'd loved running his thumbs across those high cheekbones and that round, stubborn chin. He'd been addicted to her wide, sexy mouth, with its full lips, and he'd adored her curly, black-as-coal hair. Tanna's skin, thanks to her Bengalese grandmother always made her look like she'd recently returned from a six-week holiday in the hot Caribbean sun.

Tanna was warm island breezes and hot beach bonfires, with a body made to wear a bikini, or better yet, nothing at all. She was a hot sun, a shooting star, blue skies, happiness.

Or she had been…

Before she screwed with his life and made him look like an idiot in front of his family and the world. Before she'd left and his world spun out of control.

He didn't need to see her again, didn't need to hear whatever the hell it was she wanted to say. He'd worked damned hard at surviving her, creating a life he loved and enjoyed, and he'd made a conscious effort to forget her. Like Ray, she'd caused chaos in his life and he never again wanted to feel like he was falling out of an airplane without a parachute.

He was over her.

He had to be.

"What the hell are you doing here, Tanna?" he demanded in a low growl.

"I need to talk to you," Tanna said, advancing into the room and standing next to an easy chair, a twin to the one he was sitting in. He saw her eyes flitting to his leg and an exquisitely arched eyebrow lifted. "What happened?"

"My dirt bike and I parted ways," Levi responded curtly. He jerked his head, hoping she didn't notice the fine tremor in his hands. "You know the way out."

Tanna ignored his order and sat down on the chair, placing her tote bag on the floor next to her. She rested her forearms on her knees and clasped her hands together. "We need to talk, Levi."

Did he want to hear anything she had to say? Hell no. And hell yes.

Hell no, because her walking out on him shortly before their wedding without an explanation made him reluctant to indulge in a rehash ten-plus years later. And hell yes, because, dammit, this was Tanna. The only woman who'd ever caused his lungs to stop functioning, blood to drain from his brain, his heart to beat erratically.

Self-reliant and reticent, Levi didn't make friends easily and, before Tanna Murphy, had never been in love. For months after her leaving, he'd felt like his ribs were broken, every breath he took hurt.

He'd loved her, craved her, would've moved heaven and earth for her. And, because of who he was, his nonmarriage had made all the papers on the East Coast. And on the West Coast too.

God, he'd been the village idiot.

"Just walk your pretty ass out of here, Murphy."

Tanna tipped her head and Levi noticed the determination in her eyes. Dammit. He recognized her look; he'd seen enough of it when she was injured in an accident of her own, before their engagement. Tanna didn't take no for an answer. And since he couldn't forcibly remove her from his house, he was stuck listening to her.

Levi scowled at his right leg resting on a small ottoman. She pretty much had a captive audience and that annoyed the ever-loving crap out of him.

But if he was going to listen to whatever drivel she was about to spout, he'd get something out of it. He narrowed his eyes at her. "You can have five minutes if you make me a cup of coffee."

"Fifteen minutes."

"Ten minutes, but for that I want coffee and a sandwich," Levi countered.

Tanna had the audacity to smile at him. "Or I could do neither and just sit here and stare at you until you give in."

Levi picked up his phone and waved it. "Or I could call 911 and charge you for trespassing."

He saw her hesitate and heard the silent curse on the tip of her tongue. She opened her mouth to speak, hesitated and snapped her mouth closed.

"I thought you'd see it my way," Levi said as she stood up. "You'll find everything you need in the kitchen. And do not think you can fob me off with a PB&J. There's deli meat, salad stuff and an array of condiments. Pile it on, princess."

Tanna stiffened at the use of her old nickname, the one he used to murmur with affection. Now it was coated with sarcasm and a whole lot of annoyance. He'd made sure of it.

Levi watched Tanna walk out of his study and pushed both his hands through his hair. He really wanted a sandwich, mostly so he could take a pain pill, but he was willing to put up with the pain if it meant her walking out of his house and his life.

Tanna Murphy had a way of complicating the hell out of everything and all he craved was simplicity.

Tanna Murphy found the kitchen off the hallway and immediately walked up to the overlarge fridge and rested her forehead against the cool double doors, try-ing to control her breathing. Her rental car was parked in his driveway and she fought the urge to walk back through the house, out the front door and drive back to Beacon Hill or, even better, to Logan International Airport.

You promised yourself you would do this, Murphy.

She'd sworn to herself she'd do anything to combat the PTSD symptoms that had suddenly flared up be-fore she left London. It was easy to identify the trigger; she'd been the first responder to a car accident where a dark-haired, dark-eyed teenager had caused a multi-car pileup. The girl had looked like Addy, and Tanna had frozen. After a minute, her colleague had yanked her off the patient and provided the medical treatment necessary, and Tanna, from that minute, started suffering from anxiety attacks and flashbacks to her own car accident.

She was put on medical leave and, on the advice of her London-based therapist, she'd returned to Boston to face her past. But to her friends and family, she was taking a break from work. Her overprotective brothers didn't need to hear about the demons she was fighting.

Tanna walked across the black-and-white tiles of the kitchen to pull out a chair at a big wooden table. She'd sit here for a minute, gather her courage, because, damn, she needed it. She had to confront the past in order to return to work, to do her damn job. Nobody needed an EMT who hyperventilated in a crisis.

Tanna had only been back in Boston for a week and her local therapist, located in the very trendy area of Back Bay, already had her talking through her memories of the accident. She'd accompanied Tanna on her visit to the scene of the fatal crash, and wanted her to talk to the people impacted by the accident. Isla, having lost her only child, Addy, in the same accident, had been the first person on Tanna's list.

Their conversation had not gone well.

Tanna blinked away her tears. Addy had been bright and beautiful and so damn conscientious. She'd been working her way through college, juggling two jobs and her studies with grace and humor. The night of the accident was the first night in months she'd allowed herself to have some fun.

And, yes, it was stupidly unfair that Addy, completely sober, the most mature and responsible person in their group of friends, was the one who'd lost her life in the crash. And Isla felt the same. Tanna could see Isla's point—Addy, poor but proud, had been studying to be a social worker and worked at soup kitchens and no-kill animal shelters in her spare time. Tanna, a trust fund baby, paid little attention to her studies but was completely devoted to all-night partying with her friends. Addy had been driving Tanna's car because Tanna was drunk, and Addy, an inexperienced driver, hadn't been able to handle the powerful convertible.

Tanna didn't blame Isla for being angry; the useless society girl survived when sweet Addy hadn't. And Tanna'd not only survived, but in the hospital she'd fallen in love with the guy who'd been driving behind them, who'd held her hand while they waited for medical assistance to arrive. The same guy who also happened to be the son of a famous billionaire.

And then Levi had slid a diamond onto her finger.

She'd been told she was exceptionally lucky to be alive, even luckier her family had resources for her recovery.

Because, as Isla had pointed out, she was the lucky one, the girl who'd cheated death, who'd come out of a terrible situation with a couple of scars and a gorgeous man on her arm.

Hell, Isla was right…

And that was why she'd run away from her privileged lifestyle and her wonderful fiancé ten years ago, because the only way she could deal with the guilt of surviving when Addy hadn't was to be anything but that party-loving, credit card flashing trust fund baby. She owed it to Addy to be better, to be more, to contribute…

To suffer.

Tanna sighed, digging both sets of fingers into her hair. Her conversation with Isla had been brief and unpleasant but it was over. Now she needed to talk to Levi…

He looked good, Tanna admitted. If she ignored his pale face and his dinged body, he looked…wonderful. At twenty-four he'd been tall and built and, sure, conventionally handsome with his deep brown hair shot with auburn and his ink-blue eyes. But somehow, and unfairly, Levi Brogan looked even better a decade later. He seemed a lot more muscular and more masculine, with heavy scruff on his face and messy hair.

Unfortunately, her ex-fiancé, even battered and bruised and a little broken, was wildfire hot.

So unfair.

Tanna rubbed her hands over her face and tipped her head back to look at the wooden beams running across the ceiling. Running out on Levi, hurting him, still shamed her, it was her biggest regret.

She'd left his engagement ring on the hall table of the house in Beacon Hill, along with a letter addressed to him in a sealed envelope. She could've explained she was debilitated with guilt, having second thoughts about getting married so young, that she wasn't ready to be anyone's wife.

That she had a debt to pay, that she needed to do more, be more. For Addy.

She could've said she was wondering if she was confusing gratitude with love…

She could've written any or all of that, but she didn't. Through tears, and with her heart breaking, she'd just said she was sorry and she couldn't marry him.

Tanna didn't regret not getting married, didn't regret, not for one moment, the last ten years, but she did regret hurting Levi, for running when she should've had the guts to face him.

But she'd been scared…

Scared she'd never be anything more than her brothers' adored, overly protected sister, Levi's wife, a socialite with ample funds who loved art and designer clothes.

She'd wanted to be more…

More grounded, more real. She'd wanted to be a person who gave rather than took.

And, in time, she'd hoped to feel less guilty. But that had yet to happen.

Tanna doubted it ever would. So, she would work at what she could control and that included facing the past, dealing with her PTSD and getting back to work…

"Hell, Murphy, are you baking the damned bread? What's taking so long?" Levi bellowed.

…and making Levi a damned sandwich.

Two

Standing in his light-filled office, Carrick Murphy, the oldest of the four Murphy siblings, looked across his desk to his two brothers. Finn, as per usual, was on his smartphone, occasionally sipping from his *Nerd? I prefer intellectual badass* coffee mug, a gag gift from their sister, Tanna, many Christmases ago. Carrick transferred his gaze to Ronan, who was staring out the window, his thoughts a million miles away.

Carrick ran a hand through his dark hair and rubbed his hand over his jaw. He knew many Bostonians looked at them, three bachelor brothers—rich and reasonably good-looking—and their beautiful little sister, and thought they lived charmed lives. From the outside looking in it was easy to forget they'd lost their parents when they were young, that the brothers had jointly raised their younger sister and they'd all lived through Tanna's near-fatal accident. Carrick's marriage had imploded, Ronan's wife died, Finn and Beah divorced, and Tanna left Boston...

People seldom looked behind the wealth and success...

Carrick, annoyed by his introspection when he had work to do, rapped his knuckles on the desk. Two sets of Murphy green eyes focused on him. "Before we get to work, let's discuss Tanna."

"Something is up with her," Ronan said, turning around.

Carrick nodded. "I think so too."

"I have to wonder why she's really back in town because Tanna doesn't do vacations." Ronan walked over to the coffee machine. He placed a cup under the nozzle and pushed the start button. Carrick drained his cup and passed it to Ronan for a refill. "And why does she have to live in London? She can save lives here as easily as she could there."

"We can't pressure her to move back to Boston. That'll just make her run in the opposite direction," Finn said, placing his forearms on top of a stack of paper folders. "She's more stubborn than all of us put together."

Stubborn and determined. Those two traits were the only reasons she was walking after the best specialists in the country had given her a ten percent chance of regaining her mobility. A decade later, nobody would suspect their fit and active sister had spent five months in the hospital after the ball of her right femur shattered her pelvis and her left ankle splintered into what they called a fountain break. The only clues to the hell she'd endured were a few livid scars and a barely there limp.

"Does Levi know she's back?" Finn asked.

Carrick raised his shoulders. "I don't know."

"Should we give him a heads-up?" Ronan asked, thinking of their close friend.

Levi and the Murphy brothers had stayed friends after his breakup with Tanna, but Levi never spoke about their vibrant and gorgeous sister, refused to look at the many pictures of her in the Murphys' Beacon Hill house. By the way he now acted, nobody would suspect that, at one time, Levi had loved Tanna.

While they were all tight with Levi, he and Carrick had the closest relationship. And as Carrick was the eldest, being the bearer of news, both good and bad, was his responsibility. "I'll tell him." He picked up his phone and dialed his friend's number. Putting the call on speaker, he waited for Levi's terse greeting.

"Yo."

Carrick exchanged a wry smile with Ronan. Levi was taciturn and abrupt and never used three words when one would do.

Carrick opted to shoot from the hip, the way Levi preferred. "Just a call to let you know Tanna is back in town and she'll be here for about six weeks or so."

Levi waited a beat before he responded. When he did, his tone was colder than an Arctic blizzard. "Too late. She's here."

Carrick heard the call disconnect and shook his head. He took the coffee Ronan held out to him and sighed. "Levi should really stop wearing his heart on his sleeve."

Ronan smiled at Carrick's sarcasm. "Yep. And he really shouldn't be so open and forthcoming." Ro leaned back against the credenza and crossed his foot over his ankle. "Well, he's been told. That's all we can do."

"I have news…" Finn stated after a moment's silence. "And it's big."

Happy to get off the subject of his sister's and best friend's nonrelationship, Carrick turned his attention to Finn. His younger brother was normally the definition of cool and collected, so the excitement on his face was strange to see.

"As you know, Isabel Mounton-Matthews left her entire estate to Keely Matthews and to Joa Jones, whom she took in when Joa was fourteen. Keely and Joa have decided to sell most of Isabel's extensive collection to raise funds for Isabel's foundation and we are handling the sale."

The company they'd jointly inherited, Murphy International, was one of the most exclusive auction houses in the world, renowned for the quality and rarity of the pieces of art passing through their hands. The sale of Isabel's well-documented art collection would be one of the biggest in the past decade and the items were causing a stir in their wealthy art and auction circles. "I've been cataloging the collection and I've come across three paintings I think might be sleepers—"

Carrick exchanged a quick, excited look with Ronan.

A "sleeper" was an artwork whose real value or attribution had been missed by either the owner or art dealers.

"Keely said that Isabel thought it was painted by Winslow Homer. Two are iffy but there's one that makes me think it might be."

"Provenance?" Ronan asked. In their world, provenance was everything.

Finn shook his head. "There's nothing but Isabel's suspicions. But, damn, the painting I saw, stylistically, looked like it might be one of his depictions of African American rural life."

"A lost Winslow Homer?" Homer was one of the country's most revered artists and a lost painting by him would set the art world on fire. Carrick would get excited but he also knew fraudsters loved to fake Homer. And they were good at it. "It sounds too good to be true."

Ronan looked at Finn, who was their resident art historian. "Are you going to chase this down?"

"I'd love to but I'm slammed. And I think we need an expert in nineteenth-century American painters." Finn gestured to Carrick's phone. "If the paintings are by Homer, it would have to be authenticated by you-know-who."

You-know-who, she-who-should-not-be-named, Satan's Bride.

Also known as his ex-wife.

Tamlyn had written the catalogue raisonné, the definitive work detailing all of Winslow Homer's work. If Tamlyn didn't believe the paintings were by Homer, the canvas wouldn't be worth diddly-squat.

"We need a specialist art detective, preferably someone Tamlyn trusts, to run the tests, to track down any provenance," Finn stated. "Tamlyn takes every opportunity to smear your name, Carrick. She's vindictive enough to dismiss these paintings just because you brought them to her attention. But if we hire someone she respects, someone she works with regularly, we might have a shot of getting a decent result."

Carrick and Tamlyn's marriage had been brief. It was a relationship he now deeply regretted. They'd both been ridiculously unhappy and when, after a year, he'd asked for a divorce, Tamlyn punished him by dragging his reputation through the court of public opinion. Since he'd never, not once, publicly defended himself, Carrick, in certain social circles, was still considered to be a bad husband at best, an adulterer at worst.

Good thing he didn't give a crap what people thought.

At least his reputation as an honest art dealer and auctioneer was still intact, and that was all that mattered.

"Okay, point taken." He looked at Finn. "Find me an art detective whose opinion Tamlyn Smith respects."

"I'll find someone," Finn told him and then his mouth curved into a smile. "And that's Tamlyn Smith-Murphy to you, son."

Carrick resisted the urge to punch his youngest brother. Finn was yanking his chain and he'd learned not to respond. But he wished Tamlyn would stop using his surname, dammit. Yeah, she was an art appraiser and in the art world using the name Murphy added gravitas. But surely, when you'd screwed a guy six

ways to Sunday—physically, emotionally, financially
and mentally—you forfeited the right to use his name?

Carrick looked at Finn and ignored his building
headache. "Find someone with impeccable references
and unimpeachable references. The sooner we estab-
lish provenance, the more publicity we can generate
for the sale."

Ronan nodded. "This sale is going to be huge."

Carrick agreed. "And profitable."

Tanna put the plate holding two thick sandwiches
on the small table next to Levi's chair and picked up a
state-of-the-art tablet to make way for his large mug of
coffee. Levi immediately lifted the cup to his mouth,
his low groan reminding her of the sound he'd made
the few times they kissed.

For two people who'd been about to legally and mor-
ally bind themselves to each other for the rest of their
lives, they hadn't indulged in a lot of public displays of
affection. Or even private displays of affection.

For the first few months of their relationship, she'd
been in too much pain, and when she started to feel better, Levi had treated her like spun sugar. On leaving the
hospital, she'd still needed time to recover and when
she regained most of her mobility, she was so confused about what she was feeling she'd asked Levi if
they could wait until their wedding night to make love.

He'd gently teased her for being old-fashioned and
she'd felt guilty because her morals had nothing to
do with her decision. She was having enough doubts

about her future without sex complicating her thought processes.

Not making love to Levi, not having him be her first, was one of her most profound regrets.

Pulling her attention off the past—she'd have to address that soon enough—she looked around the room.

She'd visited this house a few times between leaving the hospital and running out on Levi. His parents—lovely Callie and charismatic Ray—had lived in it back then and Tanna had fallen in love with the open plan, light-filled, spacious mansion.

Callie had filled the rooms with a mishmash of contemporary and family pieces, effortlessly combining old and new into rooms that felt both lived in and cozy, comfortable and sophisticated. While this was now Levi's home, it still held traces of his mom's creative flair.

Tanna couldn't help thinking that if she'd stuck around, this might've been her home too, stamped by her style. There would be photos of her siblings on the walls along with his, artwork she'd loved and bought, pieces of furniture she'd inherited from her parents. But everything she owned was in her flat in London, Levi's stuff was here and they hadn't had the chance to combine their lives and possessions.

Because she'd run...

"I like this room," she said, ignoring his deep scowl. "It's not filled with priceless pieces of artwork like your childhood home but it's okay."

As auctioneers and fine art dealers, her family, going back generations, had amassed an incredible collection of art, most of which adorned the walls of the house in Beacon Hill. Her bedroom held a sketch by Degas and a watercolor by Georgia O'Keeffe.

She'd grown up surrounded by incredible art, textiles and ceramics, and had planned to follow her brothers into the family business at Murphy's, joining the auction house's PR and publicity department. But she hadn't been back to Boston in years and hadn't, not since her accident, been back to Murphy's. She'd avoided it because it had once been her second home, a place she adored...

Murphy's was the one place in Boston where she'd felt completely at ease and happy. She adored art, in all its forms, loved talking about it and promoting it, and being around people who loved it as much as she did. On every visit home, Tanna knew that if she stepped into Murphy International she'd start questioning her decision to become an EMT. So she avoided the family business. And, as much as she could, Boston.

Tanna sighed. "I should've just stayed in London," she said, mostly to herself.

"I absolutely agree. Feel free to go back."

She would if she could but that wasn't possible until she had her PTSD symptoms under control. And who knew how hard she'd have to work or how long it would take her to achieve that goal? Tanna's stomach clenched and the muscles in her neck contracted.

Relax, Tanna.

Concentrating on her breathing, she pushed away her negative thoughts.

She'd just hit a bad patch and she needed a little

time to get her head sorted. Her accident had been a long time ago and she was fit and healthy. She was done being hostage to her fears. She liked emergency medicine, and the notion of helping others as she was once helped was important to her.

She owed those paramedics for saving her life—her heart had stopped twice en route to the hospital—and the only way she could show her gratitude for walking away from the crash with nothing more than a few scars was to pay it forward.

Unfortunately, paying that debt came with panic attacks, flashbacks and cold sweats. She just needed to control her reactions at work. She'd live with her PTSD symptoms if she could save lives. The symptoms wouldn't, after all, kill her. Sometimes it just felt like they would.

They couldn't sit here in silence, so Tanna attempted to initiate conversation. "I'm sorry about your dad, Levi. I know it happened years ago, but I'm still sorry."

"As you said, it was a long time ago."

Okay, then. She'd try again. "And I read somewhere your family sold your dad's company when he died. It must've been difficult losing your dad and the company."

"Not really."

She hoped he was referring to the loss of the company and not his father's death. The Levi she remembered was private and reticent but he'd never been a jerk.

"Is there a point to this inane conversation? Since you walked out on me, I didn't think you particularly cared about my life. And I, in turn, don't care how you've spent the last ten years, Tanna."

"I'm an EMT." Seeing the quick flash of surprise in his eyes, she blurted out a question and immediately regretted letting the words fly. "You didn't, just once, ask my brothers where I was, what I was doing?"

"You bailed on me, bailed on the life we planned, so I didn't feel the need to keep up with yours," Levi shot back. So that was a no then.

"Sit down, say what you want to say and then leave."

His casual order, and his expectation that he would be instantly obeyed, annoyed her. Unless she was at work being paid to take orders, she took umbrage at being told what to do.

Tanna took her time walking to a wingback chair, crossing her legs, making herself comfortable. Levi placed his plate on the arm of his own chair and picked up his sandwich. "Talk. Make it quick."

Tanna stared down at her hands. She'd imagined this meeting so often, had practiced what to say, but now those carefully crafted words wouldn't come. Seeing Levi's impatience building, she forced them across her tongue. "I didn't leave you at the altar, but it was close."

"You left straight after the rehearsal dinner. A scant twenty-four hours before," Levi said, dumping his hardly touched sandwich back onto the plate and putting it on the table. Tanna forced herself to meet his eyes, a deep blue that defied description. Sometimes they were cobalt, sometimes ink. Sometimes, like now, they held more than a touch of ice.

"I should not have left without talking to you, without a goodbye. Without an explanation."

"No argument from me."

"Levi, from the time we got engaged, I had my doubt—"

"Did I ask you for an explanation? Do I want one? I have a one-word answer…no."

Well, okay then. Tanna wasn't sure what came next, so she sat quietly, wondering how quickly he'd ask her to leave. The words were on his lips; she could see them hovering there. She needed to speak before he kicked her out.

"I was wrong, and I should've had the courage to face you, to explain. It was easier to run, to leave you that letter."

"Yeah, after watching you fight to recover from your injuries, watching you learn to walk again, I was surprised by your lack of bravery. And decency."

Ouch. Tanna felt the knife in her back, felt it turn. But she couldn't argue with his statement. How she wished she could tell him the truth. That she couldn't talk to him face-to-face before she left because if she had, she knew he would have brushed off her fears as prewedding jitters. He would've dismissed her concerns, persuaded her they were doing the right thing, and she would have listened. Then she'd have been miserable. And furious with herself for not standing up to him.

"My mom canceled the wedding, called everyone and returned the presents. Christmas was pretty crap that year." Levi's words drove the knife in deeper and harder. "But we did make headlines, day after day, week after week. All of us—me, my parents, your brothers and my sisters—lived with the press following us everywhere, shoving cameras into our faces, demanding an explanation, a comment, something. Yeah, best Christmas ever."

Tanna winced. She'd asked about the press attention but Carrick told her not to worry about it and she hadn't. Because she'd been trying to find a new life, a new normal, she'd done as he suggested.

"Maybe one day you will let me explain…"

"Don't hold your breath," Levi told her, his expression reminding her of the Bering Sea in the dead of winter.

Tanna nodded and rubbed her damp hands on her thighs. "Well, I am sorry. I wish there was something I could do to make it up to you."

Levi stared at her and she could see his agile mind working, spinning a hundred miles a minute. He was cooking up something and Tanna looked at the media room door, her inner *oh-no* radar telling her to leave, now. Whatever Levi was going to say next was going to flip her life on its head.

"Carrick said you are in town for six weeks. Is that right?"

She was due to go back to work on March 1. "Give or take," Tanna replied, wondering where he was going with this.

Levi's smile was full of sarcasm. "You say you want to make it up to me?"

Yeah, and she'd meant it, kind of. She'd meant it

in an it's-the-right-thing-to-say way, not in an I'll-do-anything-to-make-it-up-to-you way.

"Uh…what do you have in mind?"

Levi picked up his coffee mug again and looked at her over the rim. "It pains me to admit this but it's become abundantly clear I need help. I'm mobile but walking hurts like hell—"

"It should if you broke your patella."

"The cast I can handle. It's annoying but manageable. But I can't hobble around because using the crutches hurts like hell. So, it would help to have a runner, a gopher. Someone at my beck and call. Someone I don't mind ordering around—" Levi bared his teeth "—because she owes me."

Oh, crap. She'd walked right into that one.

Three

Damn right, she owed him.

Tanna owed him for walking out on their engagement, from running away from their wedding, leaving behind the life they'd planned. He didn't care about the hours he'd spent by her bedside, holding her while she cried—from pain and from frustration—

Those were his choices and he lived by them.

But it had been her choice to say yes to his proposal, to agree to a Christmas wedding, to say yes when she really meant no.

The weeks and months after their nonwedding had been hell on so many different levels. He'd shrugged off the embarrassment factor and ignored the subtle comments about his young bride's flight, the fake sympathy in the eyes of people who cared more about gossip than they did about him. He'd hated the media attention for making him, as intensely private as his father was extroverted, a public spectacle.

And he never gave the money he spent on the wedding another thought.

But Tanna damn well owed him for encouraging him to take a chance on her when he knew how risky taking chances could be.

She owed him for the sleepless nights he'd spent questioning his own judgment, for making him think asking her to marry her wasn't a smart decision. For the months and years he'd spent second-guessing himself. For whipping the entire situation out of his control…

She.

Owed.

Him.

And yeah, he could freely admit he really wanted to sleep with her, still. Maybe more now than he ever had before. A decade had transformed her from an eager-to-please girl into a fully confident woman and he didn't feel the need to rein in his responses, to choose his words.

Tanna could give as good as she got.

And, hey, she was stunning and he was injured, not dead.

Levi rubbed his hand over his face, conscious of his throbbing shoulder, leg and, yeah, cock. In the past, he'd never allowed their physical interactions to go much beyond a couple of light kisses. It wasn't that he didn't desire her; he'd been twenty-four years old and a vibrating hormone, and she'd been a beautiful, striking girl.

But she'd also been broken, and every time he'd wanted to take their physical relationship deeper, he remembered her pinned to that crumpled car seat, her green eyes wide with shock and pain, her thin voice asking him if she was going to die. He clearly recalled telling her not to look at Addy, sitting in the driver's seat, slumped over the wheel, bloody and unresponsive.

During the weeks and months following that god-awful night, he'd found himself falling deeper and deeper, entranced by Tanna's fierce courage. He'd loved her, craved her and promised himself he wouldn't push her for a physical relationship. He was a big guy, he outweighed her by a hundred pounds and a part of him was terrified he'd inadvertently do something to hamper her recovery. So, he'd pushed down his desire and banked his lust. Things would change when she left the hospital...

But they hadn't. When she was finally discharged, sporting his ring, she asked for more time, to delay intimacy until they were married.

In hindsight, that was a pretty big clue all was not well.

Tanna wasn't weak now, or fragile. And the lust he'd felt for her back then was a baby version of the hot, needy, roiling emotion coursing through his system today. She was toned, healthy, vibrant and he knew she could handle him...

Physically, emotionally, mentally.

Unlike a decade ago, she was whole. And strong.

And challenging. And, God knew, he could never resist a challenge.

Payback wouldn't be a bitch, it would be a delight. Revenge would be supersweet.

Levi watched as she tried to find a way to say no, to wiggle out of her obligation. She opened her mouth and the lame excuse he expected failed to materialize. Instead, she posed a question. "How long will it take me to work off my debt?"

"Is that a yes?"

"No, it's a question," Tanna replied. "How long?"

As soon as he could use his crutches, he'd be able to fend for himself, to move about. But he still wouldn't be able to drive. And he needed to get to his businesses—his marinas, the shipyard and the extensive corporate interests he ran on behalf of the Brogan Family Trust. Yes, he could take time off work for as long as he wanted. Hell, he could retire tomorrow if he wanted to. But he didn't want to do that. Work kept him sane and by staying involved, he kept control and control was essential to his peace of mind.

"I'm not allowed to put any weight on my leg for six to eight weeks," Levi replied. "I need someone on call for another two weeks, part-time for at least another four weeks after that."

"Your sisters and mom aren't prepared to help you?" Tanna asked, looking for an escape.

"Of course they are, but I like them. I don't see why they should have to put up with my foul mood when you can."

"Because I owe you," Tanna said, sounding miserable.

Yep, she did. And also because he couldn't imagine her walking out of his life again until he knew every inch of her luscious body.

Because he wanted revenge, a little payback.

And her.

Remember that, Brogan. Sex and revenge were the only two reasons he was pushing her to stay.

Levi looked at her again and swallowed, wondering why his mouth was so dry. His heart was also slamming against his rib cage—a pissed-off prisoner demanding release—and his stomach was joining in the rebellion.

What the hell was wrong with him?

So much. He was sore, he was horny and he was, not that he'd ever admit this to anyone, a little scared. Nobody had ever affected him the way Tanna Murphy did.

Damn.

Right, enough BS, Brogan. Get your head on straight.

He was attracted to Tanna. This grown-up version of the girl he'd loved was as sexy as hell.

It was okay, normal even, to be a little carried away thinking about how she'd feel, naked and soft, and so intensely feminine, in his arms. But sex was all he'd take from her, all he had to give her. He wasn't fool enough to give her more. Not again.

"I don't think so, Levi." Tanna shook her head. "It's really not a good idea and I don't see why I should give up my…vacation time to be at your beck and call."

Why had she hesitated when she said vacation? Why

did he suspect a vacation was not the reason she was back in Boston? And why did it matter? All he needed was for her to be around…

"I'm not asking you to glue yourself to my side, Tanna. I just need you to move in here, to help with some meals, to drive me to work and back."

"You are not nearly ready to go back to work," Tanna told him, her tone as bossy as hell. Levi raised his eyebrows at her assertiveness.

"But I will be, soon. I heal fast," Levi retorted, not willing to get into an argument about something that wasn't going to happen today, or even tomorrow. "Anyway, as I was saying, I need you for a couple of hours a day, to be on call if I need you. The rest of the time will be your own."

"Good of you."

Levi refused to let her see his quick smile. Assertive and sarcastic. Better and better. And he was glad. If Tanna was the same timid, eager-to-please girl she'd been, he probably wouldn't be making this offer, wouldn't be half as interested in that version as he was in this.

At twenty-four he'd been happy to have his ego stroked; at thirty-four he liked women who pushed back, who weren't afraid to speak their minds.

He was surrounded by strong, gutsy, opinionated women and if he ever came to the point of considering another relationship—an exceedingly remote possibility—he wanted someone who could stand on her own two feet, who was prepared to make her own mistakes and live with them.

Being the voice of reason when his dad's ambition outstripped his common sense, Levi couldn't remember a time when he hadn't felt responsible for protecting his mom and sisters. When his dad died, Levi oversaw the sale of Brogan LLC and he personally managed the billions in the family trust.

He did, he admitted, have a strong rescue gene. But his mom and sisters were perfectly able to look after themselves and while they were happy for him to manage their family money, he'd been told, repeatedly, he didn't need to worry about their emotional well-being.

They had their own alpha men doing enough hovering, thank you very much.

He still felt protective of them; he probably always would. But he was smart enough not to tell them that. But they were his blood, a part of his psyche. Tanna— or any other woman—did not warrant that much of his soul. It hurt far too much when they handed it back to him, battered and bruised.

God, enough with the melodrama, Brogan.

This was a straight-up deal. He needed someone. Tanna owed him, and while he'd never be verbally abusive to her or any other woman, with her he wouldn't have to pretend he wasn't in pain, frustrated or pissed off. He could just be because, dammit, there was nothing she could do to hurt him again.

"A couple of meals, a couple of rides, a little light housekeeping, that's all I need you for." Levi shifted in his seat and pain barreled through him, digging its claws into his body, and it took everything he had not to allow her to see how weak and miserable it made him feel. He'd been vulnerable once with her. He'd never allow her to look beneath his surface again.

A tiny frown appeared between her eyebrows. "You're in pain."

Dammit, what had happened to his impenetrable mask? Not wanting to give her an inch, he made a sound he hoped sounded like a scoff. "Please."

"God save me from stubborn men," Tanna muttered.

"I'm fine, Murphy." Such a lie.

Dropping his head back, Levi fought to keep his eyes open, cursing himself for feeling so tired. Sometimes he managed to ignore the pain and drift off and he felt this might be one of those times. His battered body needed sleep to recover but he didn't want to fall asleep now, not in front of Tanna. If he did, she'd leave and he might never see her again.

He wouldn't get any payback if she did that.

Levi forced his eyes open and gripped her wrist. "Will you be here when I wake up?"

Tanna shook her head. "Probably not."

Disappointment, hot and sour, rocketed through him. Why did he care? She meant nothing to him, not anymore.

Tanna didn't try to pull her wrist from his grip and her skin was so soft, so smooth. He thought he heard her sigh and her voice, when she spoke, came from a long way away. "I have things to do. I need to talk to my brothers, explain what I'll be doing here. I'll be back in a couple of hours."

"Promise?"

"Yeah. Sleep now, Levi."

Levi hoped, for the first time in a decade, he'd see her again. But only because, he sternly reminded himself as he drifted off, he needed help and she owed him.

And because he really, really, really wanted to see her naked.

Like that other famous auction house on the other side of the pond, Murphy's boasted a canvas portico in front of its main entrance with Murphy International written in white across the bloodred canvas. It was simple, effective and attractive, and Tanna felt the familiar kick of pride as she stared up at the letters spelling her surname.

Her great-grandfather started the company, passed it on to her grandfather, then to her father and now her brothers were running the world-famous auction house with satellite offices across the world.

She was the only Murphy who'd ever stepped away, who was working in a completely different field.

The thought made her sad.

Tanna jammed her hands into the pockets of her coat, conscious of her heart beating out of her chest. Just like always, she'd planned to avoid Murphy's, but she needed to talk to Carrick and he was, if she remembered correctly, leaving for Tokyo shortly. She needed to tell him she was moving out of the Beacon Hill house, moving in with Levi…

But only to help him, of course.

She definitely could not tell her brother she hoped, as insane as it sounded, that somehow, some way, she and Levi would finally get naked and she'd find out what making love with her ex-fiancé felt like.

She'd spent many nights imagining the way his hands would feel on her skin, how strong and hard he'd be when he pushed into her, filling up those empty and desperate spaces no man had ever managed to fill.

She needed to know because, honestly, her sexual education was incomplete.

She and Levi were done, over, their time had passed…

But, not having slept with him, Tanna was convinced there was a puzzle piece missing, like she'd never quite seen the complete picture. Like she'd never read the last chapter in a sad but compelling story.

Tanna heard the incoming message on her phone and pulled it out of her pocket. She swiped the screen and read the text from Carrick.

Security just warned me about a suspicious-looking woman casing the joint. Get your ass in here before you get arrested.

Tanna grinned. She knew Murphy's security firm employed facial recognition software and she'd been identified within a few seconds of arriving at the entrance. Carrick was just yanking her chain.

Tanna greeted the doorman and walked inside the iconic building, her boots echoing on the polished concrete floor. In front of her was the concierge, and to the left and right were the main viewing rooms.

Tanna was a frequent visitor to Murphy's website and knew there was an upcoming auction of Henry

Moore sculptures and a collection of vintage clothing and accessories. She wanted to lose herself in both exhibitions but she knew she couldn't afford to step inside either room—there were too many memories here that she wasn't quite ready to deal with.

Tanna watched as a young woman wearing a black pencil skirt and sky-high red heels half ran up the marble steps leading to the private offices on the floors above. She pushed down a wave of envy. How lucky that woman was to be working here, to be interacting with art lovers, with collectors, with the beautiful objects. How fortunate she was to be immersed in art, surrounded by beauty.

She could be you. You worked here, before you left. You chose to leave, Tanna Murphy, nobody chased you away.

Tanna had left because she didn't have a right to live her dream life, the life she'd been born to. Addy'd never had that chance and it was Tanna's fault. For Addy she had to do more, be better, be useful.

Art was lovely but it wasn't important…

She shouldn't have come back here. She should've just called Carrick…

Feeling sad and emotional and teary-eyed, Tanna ran up one flight of stairs, through a security door and up another flight of stairs. Her feet took her down the hallway to Carrick's large, third-floor office and after greeting Marsha, Carrick's PA, she knocked on his partially open door.

Carrick looked up at the knock and his smile broadened as he waved her in. Standing up, he kissed her cheek and shook his head, bemused.

"Why are you looking at me like that?" Tanna asked him, dropping her bag onto one of the chairs on the opposite side of his desk.

"Just happy that I've finally gotten you to come into Murphy's. I'm also thinking about how much you look like Mom," Carrick replied, his voice gruff. Tanna appreciated the observation but she knew she couldn't hold a candle to her obscenely beautiful mother.

"I know I don't talk about her often, Tan, but I still miss her. I miss them both."

Tanna's eyes misted over. "I do too. But I don't remember them as well as you do."

Carrick gestured to his messy desk. "I could do with Dad's help today," he admitted, slapping his hands on his hips.

Tanna dropped into the other chair and crossed her long legs. "Problems?" She couldn't help asking the question. She might be completely devoted to her career but Murphy's was, and would always be, a huge part of her.

Carrick walked around his enormous desk and rested his butt against the edge. "When are there ever not?"

"Tell me."

Because, just for a minute or two, she wanted to pretend she was still part of this business, still a Murphy. Tanna never got the chance to talk art with her colleagues. For the most part, art didn't interest them and they were also too damn busy saving lives.

But she wasn't at work now and she could spend time talking about Murphy clients and collections with her elder brother.

It didn't mean anything…

"For someone who professes to have no interest in the family company, you still ask pertinent questions and make sensible suggestions," Carrick said later, sending her a sly grin.

"I could still use you here at Murphy's, in public or client relations. You enjoy people, love art and you're naturally warm and charming, just like Mom. Do you still enjoy being an EMT?" Carrick asked her before she could think of a suitable response.

Tanna crossed her legs and stared at the tip of her leather boot. "It's an important job, Carrick. I make a difference."

"You didn't answer my question," Carrick persisted. "Do you enjoy it?"

She didn't *hate* it.

She looked at the painting sitting on the easel in the corner of his office and lifted her chin. She wasn't going to spoil her trip to Murphy's by fighting with her brother over her return, something she couldn't consider. So she changed the subject. "Is that a Homer?"

Carrick, thank God, didn't push.

"We're not sure," Carrick said, looking at the painting of two children and their African American mother.

"It's an intensely powerful painting and if it isn't a Homer, then it's a superb fake."

"I have an appointment shortly with an art detective we are hiring to chase down provenance and run tests."

"I thought you employed art detectives. Isn't that what Finn does?"

"Finn is checking and double-checking the provenance of all the paintings we are putting up for sale at the Mounton-Matthews auction. It'll be the biggest sale of the decade and we've been working on it for months. Finn is slammed. We also need to use an art detective Tamlyn trusts because she'll be the one who will eventually decide whether it's a genuine Homer or not," Carrick continued.

Tanna's eyes cooled at the mention of his ex. She and Tamlyn had never jelled and neither made any bones about the fact. "You're dealing with that witch?"

It was Carrick's turn to change the subject and he did it by tapping the face of his watch with his index finger. Tanna couldn't complain; what was good for the goose and all that.

"I have an appointment in five and I need to leave for the airport in an hour so was there a reason for this visit or did you just drop in to say hi?"

Tanna scratched her forehead and wrinkled her nose. "Talking of revisiting the past…"

"Yeah?"

"So, as I said, I'm in Boston for about six weeks…" Tanna nibbled at the corner of her mouth. *Get it out, Murphy.* Her words rolled out in a rush of syllables. "I went to see Levi this morning. I wanted to apologize to him, see if I could make things right."

Carrick winced and Tanna didn't blame him. They both knew a couple of words wouldn't make it right. "How did he respond?"

"It didn't go well," Tanna admitted. "I apologized. He was dismissive."

Tanna looked past her brother's shoulder to his incredible view of the Downtown Crossing neighborhood and Boston Common.

Carrick folded his arms, tipped his head and waited for more. Because, somehow, he knew there were at least ten thousand things she wasn't saying. "He's still angry at me."

"Uh-huh?"

"He says I owe him and there's something I can do to repay him."

When Tanna didn't speak again Carrick frowned.

"You going to tell me what Brogan wants, Tan?" Carrick demanded, not bothering to hide his curiosity.

"He wants me to move in with him. He needs someone to run errands for him, cook and clean." Tanna pulled a face. "He says he can be rude to me and not care."

"Uh-huh," Carrick said and Tanna didn't appreciate his lack of effort to hide his amusement. "And you believed him?"

"He was pretty damn rude," Tanna muttered.

She couldn't see anything funny in what she'd said. What was wrong with her oldest brother?

"So, are you going to agree to his demands, clear your debt?" Carrick asked.

"You think I should?"

"I think you should help him out, Tan."

Tanna narrowed her eyes. "You're just saying that in

the hopes something will spark between us again, so there might be a chance of me moving back to Boston."

"I've never made a secret of the fact that I want you back in Boston and that I want you to be part of the family business again, part of this family. We've missed you intensely and you've barely spent any time with Ronan's kids. London is a hella long way away. Levi sat by your bedside for months. The least you can do is help him out when he's in a jam."

Yep, Carrick wasn't above playing the guilt card. Tanna muttered a curse. "Ugh."

"Is that a yes?" Carrick asked.

"Actually, I'd pretty much made up my mind to help Levi before I got here." Tanna glared at him. "But I'm not happy about it."

Carrick started to speak but was interrupted by another knock on his door. Marsha opened it and behind his middle-aged, short and ruthlessly efficient PA stood a tall blonde.

"Carrick, your three o'clock appointment is here. This is Dr. Sadie Slade." Marsha stepped aside to allow a tall, modern Cinderella look-alike to walk into his office. Tumbling honey curls framed a triangular face dominated by big, round blue eyes holding more than a trace of violet. Tanna looked from the *Sports Illustrated* model to her eldest brother and her eyes widened at the look of profound— Was that shock on his face?

It was either that or Carrick was having a heart attack. Since she knew her brother was a workout junkie, she figured she didn't need to call for an ambulance.

Thank God, because the thought of giving him mouth-to-mouth made her want to gag.

Then again, the blonde—judging by her flushed face and her inability to pull her eyes off Carrick's face—wouldn't hesitate.

Chemical reaction.

Tanna looked past Carrick to where Marsha stood in the doorway and she caught Marsha's eye, fighting not to return her grin. So, she wasn't the only one who'd caught the zings between these two.

Ha ha, karma is a bitch, Carrick.

He'd laughed at her for her Levi predicament. She couldn't wait to watch him dealing with Dr. Sadie Slade, acting like the cool, reserved CEO of one of the premier auction houses in the world while fighting his fierce attraction.

Tanna had no idea how he was going to act cool with his tongue on the floor.

Four

Tanna, leather tote over her shoulder, rapped briefly on Levi's front door and stepped inside. Pulling her suitcase into the hall, she dropped her duffel bag to the floor and looked up to see Levi shuffling down the hallway.

He stopped, stood on his good foot and relaxed his arms, regarding her with eyes that instantly made her want to spill her secrets.

Even dinged and dented, you are so hot.

I've missed you.

It's weird and wrong and right to be here.

"Hi." *Scintillating opening line, Murphy.*

"I didn't think you were coming back," Levi said, his voice extra growly. And, strangely, extra sexy.

"Miss me?" Tanna asked, aiming for jokey but hitting breathless. Honestly, what was wrong with her? She just had to look at Levi and her brains, and ovaries, exploded.

Not good.

"I survived. Just I like I survived the past decade," Levi replied, but his words didn't hold the bite she expected. He just sounded tired.

Tanna glanced at the antique, freestanding clock in the corner, wincing when she saw it was later than she'd realized. "Yeah, I'm sorry I'm a bit late. I meant to be here earlier, but I had to go see Carrick, tell him I was moving out of his house into yours—"

Alarm skittered across Levi's face. "Ah, I meant to call him, to explain the situation, but I fell asleep. How did he take the news?"

Tanna thought about her brother's reaction. She couldn't forget his amusement.

"Strangely, he said that I should help you. He, kind of, agreed that I owed you. But he didn't say very much on the subject at all."

She really hoped her big brother wasn't trying to play matchmaker. That ship had sailed.

And sunk.

Levi frowned and instantly looked suspicious. "That doesn't sound like Carrick."

"I thought so too."

Levi ran his hand over the scruff on his jaw. "Huh. Should I call him and ask?"

Tanna shook her head. Why borrow trouble? "No… hell no. Let sleeping dogs, or noncommunicative brothers, lie." She glanced down at her bags. "Where can I dump these?"

"There's a guest bedroom up the stairs on the right. I have a cleaning service. They come in once a week and they keep it in a state of readiness."

"And I supposed your overnight guests stay in your bed and don't use the guest room."

Tanna winced when the words left her mouth and she wished she could haul them back. Dammit. His sex life had nothing to do with her, nothing at all. But if he did have a live-in or a steady girlfriend, why wasn't she here, tending to her man?

And if he did have a girlfriend, how would she react to Tanna's presence in his house?

But if he *was* seeing someone, Tanna would have the perfect excuse to leave. She could just pick up her bags and walk out the front door. There was only one way to find out and Tanna bit the conversational bullet. "So, should I be worried about some girlfriend showing up here, ready to scratch me stupid?"

A smile touched Levi's mouth. "Jealous?"

She was not going to dignify that with an answer. Mostly because, yes, she was. But she was allowed to be. This man had once considered spending the rest of his life with her. But she'd left him, bailed out in a spectacular fashion. She'd forfeited her right to feel jealous.

Or any other emotion.

Tanna, because she knew she was digging a hole for herself, just lifted her chin and waited for him to answer her question, and Levi finally put her out of her misery…

Correction…to satisfy her curiosity.

"No, no girlfriend, steady or otherwise."

Her inner twelve-year-old did a happy dance. Ridiculous. Not wanting him to see a hint of her relief, she bent down to pick up her duffel bag.

"And you?"

Tanna straightened, blinked and frowned. "Me what?"

"Are you seeing someone?"

Not for a long, long time. When last had she even been on a date? How sad was it that she didn't have the foggiest idea?

"Not that it has anything to do with you but…no. Not currently."

Levi's eyes burned with dark blue intensity. "Good."

"It's not good! Why is it good?" Tanna demanded.

Levi half smiled again and gripped his crutches. "You and I, Tanna Murphy, have unfinished business, and that business would be complicated if other people were involved."

Unfinished business? What was he talking about? Was he talking about sex?

Please, please let him be talking about sex.

Levi turned his back to her and Tanna couldn't help her eyes dropping to his butt, perfectly outlined by a pair of straight-legged track pants. Utterly distracted, Tanna appreciated the way his long-sleeved T-shirt hugged his broad back and showed off his wide shoulders and skimmed over his big biceps. Man, he was as delicious going as he was coming…

As for the other type of coming, she'd like to see that too.

Levi stopped, half turned and looked back at her. Their eyes clashed and held, and Tanna watched his eyes deepen and darken. His hot gaze bounced from her eyes to her mouth and back up again.

It had been far too long since she'd kissed him. She'd forgotten what his mouth felt like, how he tasted. She needed to know…

She couldn't wait for a second longer. Tanna didn't hesitate, moving closer to him so she could place her hands on his wide chest. Keeping her eyes on his, she stood up on her tiptoes to allow her lips to touch his.

His lips felt cool under hers, firm and so damn masculine. Tanna moved her hands from his chest to hold his strong upper arms, the muscles unyielding. She wanted to pull his shirt up his chest, find hot, warm skin, but she just dug her fingertips into his flesh, disappointed he'd yet to respond to her kiss.

She was out of practice, so maybe she hadn't seen lust in his eyes, maybe she'd read him wrong. Sinking back to her toes, she dropped her hands and felt her face blaze with humiliation.

"Okay, so I misread you, this… Sorry." Tanna rocked on her heels. Embarrassed beyond belief, Tanna turned, but Levi grabbed the hem of her jacket, stopping her flight.

Tanna tossed her hair back and lifted her head, forcing herself to meet his eyes. Before she could, he hauled her into him, his flat hand on her lower back pulling her close. His hand was strong, his erection felt like a shaft of pure, hard delight and his mouth—finally—was on hers and doing what his mouth did best.

And that was kissing her…

She remembered his banked and restrained kisses from long ago, but this was a different Levi kissing her. This Levi wasn't polite or thoughtful. His mouth demanded she respond, that she step into the fire with him and burn.

Tanna was all too happy to feel the flames. His tongue pushed past her teeth to swirl around hers and Tanna whimpered, feeling hot and scratchy and wonderful and uncomfortable, all at the same time.

This was a grown-up kiss, sexy, raunchy, demanding. It was a kiss shared by a man and a woman, different but equal. It was an I-want-you kiss, a this-will-only-get-better kiss. It was bourbon and ice, deep midnight, the shock of a dip in icy water, the thrill of free diving.

It was Levi let off his leash.

Tanna felt his fingers on her neck, skimming the shell of her ear and traveling over her cheekbone. Then his hand dropped, and he returned his grip to the crutch he'd tucked under his arm. Tanna stepped back, pushed her fingers into her hair before dropping her hand to hold his crutch, needing a little support of her own.

Only Levi Brogan could make her feel unsteady.

"What the hell was that?" she demanded, the words husky.

"That was the unfinished business I was talking about," Levi told her, his tone now brusque. "And, just so we are clear, part of our unfinished business is having you under me—or more likely, given my busted leg—on top of me."

"Uh…uh…" Tanna felt her head whirl, the moisture in her mouth faded. God, she wanted that. Now, immediately.

Not making love with Levi all those years ago was, along with handing her keys to Addy, one of her biggest regrets.

Tanna released a long breath. "Wow, tell me what you really think, Levi."

A small smile touched his lips. "I shoot from the hip, Tanna, and you should be prepared for that."

He lifted his hand to rake back his dark brown hair, which contained those flashes of auburn she loved so much. Tanna was also happy to see the fine tremors in his fingers, showing her he wasn't as controlled as he wanted her to think.

Levi cleared his throat and Tanna made herself look at him. "Ten years ago, I treated you like glass and you ran. This time around, I'm going to tell you what I want from you. I'm going to be as up-front as possible."

She could live with that. "Okay."

"As much as I'd love to pick you up and carry you to the nearest horizontal surface, that's not going to happen today." Humor flashed in his eyes and Tanna caught her breath as his brief smile upped his sexy factor a thousand percent.

"But in a week or two, hopefully a helluva lot sooner, I am going to ask you if you want to sleep with me and I sure as hell hope you say yes." He looked past her to the front door and his expression turned hard and remote. "A decade ago I gave you my heart. That's not on offer anymore. But my body sure as hell is." Levi adjusted his crutches under his arms. "And, no, before you ask, this is a completely separate issue from you helping me out, the debt I said you need to repay."

A million thoughts buzzed through her but one dominated: if they never made love, Tanna knew she would regret it. She would always wonder how he'd taste, feel, move.

Whether he'd fill her as wonderfully as she'd imagined or whether he'd be a letdown. If she didn't make love with him, just once, she'd regret it for the rest of her life.

He wouldn't pressure her, coerce her or nag her. No, that wasn't Levi's style. In his direct way, he'd just stated his position and thrown his offer on the table. It was hers to pick up.

Or not.

It would be easy to say yes, to allow her hot blood and the taste of him on her lips to influence her decision. Sure, she wanted this but now that her blood had cooled and she was thinking more clearly, she was a little scared and a lot uncertain.

Was she ready for this? Did she really want to reopen the door to the only man who'd ever touched her heart?

Shouldn't she think about this a little more?

Tanna jammed her hands into the pockets of her leather jacket and hunched her shoulders in what she hoped was a casual shrug.

It wasn't a yes to sex; neither was it a no. Her nonresponse left her some wiggle room.

"I won't give you my heart again either, Levi." She knew that for sure. Her heart was permanently off-limits.

Levi's cold smile held no amusement. "Tanna, you never did."

In the white-and-sunshine-yellow guest bedroom upstairs, Tanna unpacked her clothes and placed them in the closet, her toiletries and makeup in the minimalistic but pretty en suite bathroom. All the while she wondered if she'd completely lost her marbles.

Levi wasn't an idiot. He knew her nonanswer wasn't a solid no and there was a strong possibility that she'd sleep with him. Not tonight obviously, or tomorrow, but sometime in the near future.

She might as well start wrapping her head around the concept.

At some point, she'd see whether his long body was as muscled as she imagined. She'd know how he tasted, how he liked to move. Judging by the kiss they'd shared, Tanna had no doubt Levi was a skilled lover, and at the very least, she expected an orgasm. Maybe, if she was very lucky, two.

It had been a while since she'd felt comfortable enough with a guy to allow him in her bed.

Levi might be terse and abrupt, but she trusted him with her body. She had no intention of handing over her heart…because she wasn't the heart-handing-over type and also because he didn't want it.

She'd had her chance and she was fully aware she'd never get another.

Their time had passed and sex, and their insane attraction, was all that was left.

Their history couldn't be changed but when she and Levi did make love, her curiosity would finally be satisfied, and she wouldn't have to live with any more *what if?* thoughts.

Tanna looked out of the guest bedroom window onto a small lake that was part of the Lockwood Country Club's golf course. As she always did when she felt out of sorts and needed a strong dose of what was, not what she wanted to be, she called Padma.

Her godmother specialized in step-into-the-light talks. Although it was nearing midnight in London, Padma answered on the second ring, sounding alert and focused. "Baby girl."

Her mom called her baby girl and Padma's greeting created a link between her and her mom. "Hey, fairy godmother."

Tanna heard the flick of a lighter, Padma's long inhale. How she wished Padma'd give up smoking, but despite her nagging, and Tanna had done plenty, Padma had yet to give up her pack-a-day habit.

Tanna opened her mouth to pester but Padma beat her to it. "Don't start, darling. Rather, tell me why you are calling in the dead of night."

How did she explain the unexplainable? Tanna decided it was better just to give it to her straight. "I've got myself into a bit of a pickle."

Padma had been married five times and always had a man, or three, hanging off her every word. She was a master at digging herself out of deep holes. "Ooh, sounds promising. What did you do?"

Tanna smiled. Padma was the type of person who appreciated drunken mistakes, dancing on bars, protest action and fast cars. She couldn't abide mediocrity or, as she called it, "sheep behavior."

"I'm not at the Beacon Hill house with Carrick."

"Please tell me that you have found a hot man to have an affair with," Padma replied, sounding delighted. Then she hesitated, remembering Tanna wasn't the fall-into-bed-on-a-whim type. "Darling, if that's not the case, then feel free to lie. Because, as you know, I've been telling you for months and months that you need a good rogering."

Honestly, who was Roger and how did his name come to be associated with sex? Only the English...

"Well, I didn't move in because I was offered sex. That came a few hours after I barged back into his life."

It only took Padma a moment to connect the dots. "Oh, for the love of baby Jesus! You went to see Levi, didn't you?"

It was a rhetorical question since Padma knew there was only one man who could make Tanna feel so out of control.

"I presume you threw yourself at his feet and demanded forgiveness?" Padma's question was scathing.

"I wasn't subservient! I asked him for forgiveness, he told me I owed him, that I needed to help him and that he wanted to sleep with me." Tanna wrinkled her nose. Those were the highlights, weren't they? So much had happened today.

"Oh, my God, you are too much."

Okay, that wasn't a compliment. Not waiting for Padma, Tanna quickly explained the situation. When she was done, Tanna heard Padma light up another cigarette and waited for her pronouncement. "Sounds like a bad idea, darling girl."

The hell of it was that she was right.

Tanna transferred her phone to her other ear, lifted her foot up onto the seat and hooked her elbow around her knee.

"I saw him, and I knew I needed to be here, needed to do this," Tanna admitted. "It was the same feeling I had ten years ago. Back then, my gut instinct told me to run, to leave Boston. This time it's telling me to stay here with Levi. But only for the next six weeks, that's all," she quickly added. Because there was no way she'd considered returning to Boston, living here, with or without Levi.

In London she wasn't Tanna Murphy, a trust fund baby, heir to one of the oldest businesses in the city. In London she was just Murphy, another EMT trying to save lives, earning a paycheck and paying off her debt to the universe for letting her live.

For sparing her when Addy died.

"You told me, when I arrived in London, sobbing and scared, that my intuition was the most powerful part of me. It was my soul talking. You have even suggested it can be our connection to feminine wisdom, to people who have passed before us," Tanna gabbled. "I can't just dismiss what I am feeling."

"Yeah, yeah, sounds like me," Padma admitted,

irritated. "In my defense, I probably had four too many G&Ts at that stage."

Tanna grinned. Padma would move heaven and earth for her but hated it when she got sentimental and mushy. And Padma loathed it when Tanna became overly emotional or verbose.

"So, you are going to stay with him?" Padma asked.

"Yeah."

"Did you call me to ask my permission?" Padma demanded. "Last I heard, you were an adult and made your own decisions. Decide what you want to do and then do it, Tanna. Stop overanalyzing it to death."

And that was why she'd called. Right there…that. Padma always said something to clarify Tanna's thinking and the words were exactly what she'd been waiting for.

So, to break it down…what did she want?

She wanted to give Levi a hand—she did owe him for leaving so abruptly and the chaos she'd caused—and she wanted to sleep with him. She'd satisfy her curiosity about sex with him and then she'd move on, back to London, back to her real life.

There! Sorted. Tanna closed her eyes and wished she could hug her godmother. And her best friend. "Thanks, Pad. Love you."

"Yeah, yeah, whatever."

Tanna heard the emotion under the irritation and decided to ramp up her godmother's annoyance. "I love you to the moon and back. I miss you so—"

Click, call disconnected.

Tanna grinned and tossed her phone onto the huge

double bed. Linking her arms around her bent knees, she remembered Padma asking her why she'd run out on her wedding, Levi, her family and her hometown. All she could tell Padma at the time was that she knew she needed to leave, that staying was impossible.

She couldn't tell her that living the pampered and protected life Levi and her brothers had mapped out for her was impossible, knowing Addy was dead.

Had she stayed and married Levi, she probably wouldn't have been miserable. She would've been a young wife with a husband who adored her, living a lovely life as one only could when one had access to enormous wealth, both his and hers. They would've been fine for a year, two, maybe three or four. But, at some point, she would've started to question her actions, to look back on her choices and wonder if marrying Levi was the best choice she could have made.

She'd made the right choice to run. She had.

Despite the fact that she been confused and guilt-ridden, and so sad, leaving Boston had been the biggest gift she'd given herself. In running, she'd discovered who she was, or could be. She'd left Princess Tanna behind and become a different person, had many different experiences—both good and bad—and looked at the world through her own lens and not one tinted by her family's or her partner's views and expectations. She'd experienced the highs and lows of life, stood on her own two feet, made her own way. Ignoring her massive trust fund, she lived on her salary, counting pennies when her bank account didn't stretch as far as she needed it to.

She'd compromised on where and how she lived, made friends and lost others, but through it all, she'd made choices for herself without taking a man's opinion into consideration. Some of those decisions had been smart, some not…but they were all part of her steep learning curve.

If she had married Levi, her Boston-based learning curve would've been gentler, softer, not as dramatic. And possibly not as much fun. It would've also been drawn by Levi, by her brothers. And, had she stayed in this city, she wouldn't be half as confident, and she'd be far less assertive.

Levi, then and now, was strong-willed, and she now realized he needed a strong woman, someone mentally tough, someone who could stand up to him, argue her point. He needed an equal partner, someone who challenged him. Young Tanna had not been that person and, if she'd stayed, would not have grown into the type of woman Levi, deep down, wanted. Needed.

Despite having hurt Levi, despite leaving a mess behind her, not getting married had been the correct thing to do. Oh, maybe she could've handled the breakup better, maybe she should've stuck around and cleaned up her own mess, but she hadn't and that was on her. She'd apologize for how she did it but not for the action itself.

So, what was she expecting from Boston this time around? To face her past so she could heal. Good sex, at some point, would be a bonus. To pay off her debt to Levi by helping him out.

But nothing else had changed.

She was only going to stay in Boston as long as it

took her to put her past into perspective and deal with the PTSD symptoms. She could not go back to London still fighting her demons. She needed to get them, once and for all, under control.

Because HART—Hazardous Area Response Team— was a vital service and she and her colleagues took on the worst cases and the trickiest situations. But she couldn't return to the unit if she wasn't a hundred percent psychologically healthy. She owed that to herself and to her colleagues but mostly to her patients. She'd had the best care possible when she was injured and she believed that her patients deserved the best of her. So she needed to stay in Boston, confront her past, see her therapist. Help Levi out and clear her debt. Then she'd go back to London and her demanding, important job.

That was her plan and she was sticking to it.

After washing her face and refreshing her lipstick, Tanna headed back downstairs, and as her foot hit the bottom stair, she heard feminine voices in the kitchen. If she wasn't mistaken, and she didn't think she was, Levi's sisters were in the room, ready to ambush her.

Tanna bit her lip, debating whether to face his family or run upstairs and hide. Uncertain as to what she should do, she froze in place, her mind whirling. She hadn't spent much time with the twins when she and Levi were together. His sisters had been away at college and only came home for their brother's engagement party. Jules and Darby, and their friend DJ, were outwardly friendly but Tanna wasn't a fool. She'd immediately realized she would have to work hard to prove to them she was worthy of their brother.

The problem was that by the time she met them she wasn't sure whether she wanted to prove anything to them. And she wasn't sure she wanted to face them now. Tanna, hoping no one had heard her clattering down the stairs, turned around to run back up to her room when she heard a throat clearing.

"Chicken."

God, she was so busted. By Callie Brogan of all people.

"I thought you had more gumption than that, Tanna."

She'd thought wrong. Her back to Callie, Tanna pulled a face and gathered her courage to face Levi's mom.

Tanna scrunched her eyes closed, took a deep breath and felt every muscle in her body contract. She regretted running out on Levi, she really did, but she also felt bad for never contacting Callie again.

Levi had brought his mom to the hospital, maybe two or three weeks after Tanna's accident, and ten minutes after meeting her, Tanna fell in love. Callie, blonde and blue-eyed and so tiny Tanna couldn't believe she'd produced the big and burly Levi, took her hand, kissed her cheek and looked around her hospital room.

"How much longer are you going to be in here, darling?"

At that point they hadn't been sure, so Tanna had shrugged, fighting back tears. "They said a least a few months."

"Then we have to make it look less like a jail cell," Callie had declared.

She'd returned that evening with potted plants and

soft linen, cut flowers in a crystal vase and the picture of her parents that sat on Tanna's bedside table. Magazines and her tablet were in easy reach, as were sparkling water and notebooks.

Due to work constraints, Levi and Tanna's brothers could only visit her in the evening, but Callie made friends with the nursing staff and often visited Tanna out of the official hours. During those long months in the hospital, Tanna and Callie became exceptionally close and getting Callie as a mom-in-law, as a mom— something she hadn't had for the longest time—had been an enormous tick in the reasons-to-marry-Levi column.

Tanna, knowing she couldn't stay on the stairs and that running away was impossible, turned slowly and, with heavy feet, made her way down to where Callie stood waiting, looking not a day older than she had a decade before. She wore a pair of dove-gray slacks, a black cashmere jersey and diamond studs the size of pigeon eggs in her ears. On her finger rested a pink diamond and platinum ring fully able to outshine the sun. Her blond hair hit her chin in a classic bob and bold red lipstick covered her mouth, and Tanna remembered this was the woman who'd once been the most popular hostess on Boston's A-List social scene.

Expecting to see censure in Callie's eyes and a frown on her face, Tanna was shocked when Callie held out her hands with a warm and welcoming smile.

"My darling girl." She pulled Tanna into her arms. "I've missed you so."

Tanna felt tears burning as she returned Callie's

hug, unable to believe she was getting such a wonderful welcome from the woman who, she was sure, had wanted to eviscerate her for jilting her son.

"Why are you being nice to me?" Tanna asked as Callie pulled back. "I mean, don't get me wrong, I appreciate it, but jeez, I never expected such a warm welcome."

Callie cupped Tanna's cheek with a cool hand. "Oh, don't get me wrong. I was very cross with you for a long time. But you're back and I am thrilled to see you."

Tanna needed to say something about Ray, Levi's father. He'd died a few months after she'd left, and she'd sent flowers. "I'm so sorry about Ray, Callie. He was a lovely man."

Callie nodded and grief gently touched her face before wafting away. "Thank you for the white lilies. They were lovely."

Holy crap, Callie had a good memory.

Callie tucked her hand into the crook of Tanna's elbow and steered her toward the kitchen.

"I have a new partner and he keeps me on my toes." Callie flashed a brilliant smile. "He's ten years younger than me, is seriously ripped and has quite a few tattoos."

Tanna laughed at the excitement in Callie's voice. It was obvious her new man was making her very happy, in all the ways that counted.

Callie patted Tanna's hand and kept her feet moving forward. "We have so much to catch up on. I want you to meet Mason. He's so lovely and makes me so happy. But first, you have to give the girls a chance to take a bite out of your very pretty hide."

Fabulous.

"They are interrogating Levi in the kitchen. They want an explanation about why you are back. I wouldn't mind one myself."

Callie was sweet and gracious and altogether lovely but Tanna heard the note of steel in her voice. The Brogans were a tight bunch and Levi once told her that, while they argued like crazy, they were loyal to the nth degree. If you fought with one, you fought with all.

Tanna braked, not wanting to fight with anyone.

"You might as well get it over with," Callie said on a light laugh. "Pull up your big-girl panties, darling."

"But what if I don't want to?" Tanna wailed. "What if I don't own any big-girl panties?"

"Then suck it up, sunshine," Callie said cheerfully before placing her hand between Tanna's shoulder blades and propelling her into the kitchen.

Five

Levi sat at the scarred wooden table, his hand around his coffee mug, his head angled toward the doorway, expecting Tanna to appear any moment. He knew she was on her way because there was something about how the air changed when she was near. It was almost as if the atmosphere held its breath, waiting for her to arrive.

Or maybe that was just him.

Tanna stepped into the kitchen, her hands tucked into the back pockets of her jeans. She'd shed her thigh-length leather jacket, and her thin, light-green-colored silk sweater clung to her small breasts and slim curves. With her ballerina's body, she wasn't voluptuous by any means, but to him, she was as sexy as hell.

And he couldn't believe she'd agreed to sleep with

him. Well, not in so many words, but yeah, she was still here, wasn't she? Her presence in his kitchen was proof she accepted that sleeping together—having hot, raunchy sex—was a definite possibility.

Hoo-damn-ray.

Levi leaned back in his chair and watched Tanna's glance bounce from one twin's face to the other and he was impressed by her composure. He admired her calm attitude and her courage to face his sisters.

Because his sisters could be pretty damn scary. They loved hard and they loved deeply, and hurting someone they cared about—even if he was their annoying brother—made them want to do some ass kicking.

He'd never let them tag team Tanna, but he appreciated their willingness to do so.

Levi transferred his attention to his mother, caught the speculation in her eyes and immediately dropped his gaze. Callie had a fully functioning mom-dar. She'd always been too intuitive for his own good and he didn't want her seeing anything that might give her hope there was a second chance for a happy-ever-after for him and Tanna.

There would be a happy ending, for both of them, several if he had his way. But a happy-ever-after? He didn't believe in those anymore.

Tanna broke the awkward silence in the room. "Jules and Darby, it's nice to see you again."

Such a lie, Levi thought. If she could've she would've avoided this conversation. Hell, if he'd had the choice, they wouldn't be having this conversation either, but while this house was now legally his, it was also their childhood home and the home they had all shared up until a few months ago.

Frankly, he'd need a nuclear bomb to dislodge them.

"Tanna," Darby responded, making her name sound like week-old trash.

Such fun.

Levi looked longingly at the cupboard containing his ten-year-old whiskey and wished someone would pour him a shot, or two. But he couldn't drink alcohol with the pain meds, more's the pity.

Well, if he couldn't have whiskey, he wished one of the many women in his life would get him another cup of coffee.

He opened his mouth to ask for a refill, but Darby responded before he could speak.

"I wish we could say we were happy to see you," Darby said, as forthright as ever. Jules had more tact than her twin, but probably because he was as straight-forward, Levi liked Darby's shoot-from-the-hip style. He always knew exactly where he stood with that sister. "Why are you back, Tanna?"

"And if you're back only to mess with Levi's head, then we'd like you to leave," Jules interjected, folding her arms across her chest.

"He broke his knee, not his head, so he won't be taking you back," Darby continued.

Levi started to tell her she didn't talk for him, but before he could speak, Tanna held up her hand in a silent plea. When she was sure she had the floor, she straightened her shoulders and lifted her chin. "Are you two done?" she quietly asked the twins.

Jules nodded and Darby shrugged.

"Thank you," Tanna said, her voice smooth but holding a don't-mess-with-me edge. "I'm back because I had something to say to Levi—"

"What?" Darby demanded.

Levi considered responding but decided Tanna was doing a fine job dealing with his sisters on her own.

Tanna raised her eyebrows at Darby's interruption and Darby flushed. "Sorry," she muttered. "Go on."

"Thank you," Tanna said again. After a moment of silence, she continued, "What Levi and I discussed has nothing to do with his family. That's between us. As is our arrangement. While I appreciate your protective streak, I can assure you there is no chance of a reconciliation between us—"

Her declaration was a sharp-tipped blade, stabbing him in the stomach. What the hell was the matter with him? There was no way in hell he'd give Tanna a second chance, even if she wanted one...

Which she obviously didn't.

"—but I have agreed to help him out while he recovers. The reasons behind our decision have nothing to do with you," Tanna said, moving over to the coffee machine behind where Callie was sitting. She turned her back to him and reached for a mug in the cupboard above. They all waited while the machine dispensed hot black coffee and Levi was surprised when she swapped his empty cup for the full one.

"Thanks," Levi murmured.

"Hungry?" she softly asked.

"I ordered pizza. It should be here soon," Levi told

her, embarrassed when his stomach released a low growl. He was hungry for the first time since his accident and not just for food.

He wanted this woman...

Now, here. Immediately. How soon could he get his family to leave?

"That's all very well, Tanna, but you must understand your returning to Boston sounds fishy," Darby said, breaking their stare.

Levi blinked at Darby's statement and shook his head. Right. He loved his sisters but enough was enough. Injured or not, he could fight his own battles.

He cleared his throat. "While I appreciate your concern—"

"No, you don't," Callie interrupted, laughter in her voice.

Not helping, Mom. Levi scowled at her and looked back to the twins. "I don't need you to protect me. Or to interfere in something that has nothing to do with you."

Jules and Darby both rolled their eyes. In that moment, in their disbelief, the fraternal twins looked the same.

"Our love lives had nothing to do with you but that didn't stop you from interfering," Darby pointed out.

"I never interfered," Levi stated, knowing he was on thin ice. It was true. No good deed ever went unpunished.

Damn, but he longed to feel in control again. In the past week, he'd injured himself, was housebound and his ex-fiancée was not only back in his life, but in his home. What was next? A meteor strike? A swarm of locusts?

"Pfft. What about the time you took Matt outside and threatened him if he messed with DJ?" Jules demanded.

The ice cracked. "I'm not arguing with you about this, twins." Levi lowered his voice so they had no doubt he was losing his patience. "Tanna and I have come to an understanding and I'm asking you to respect that. And her," he added.

Both Jules and Darby looked mutinous, so Levi spoke again, his tone suggesting he wasn't interested in any of their opinions. "Tanna came back and she apologized. The fact that she was willing to do that is worthy of respect."

Levi ignored the surprised look on Tanna's face, the gratitude flashing in her eyes. He didn't want her gratitude, he wanted her mouth under his, their legs and arms tangled. He wanted her naked, preferably immediately.

And the sooner his interfering family left, the sooner that could happen. He started to lift himself to his feet and just managed to swallow his yelp of pain. Yeah, damn, he'd moved too fast. And if he couldn't move, then he certainly couldn't make love to Tanna the way he wanted to, the way their first time deserved.

He wouldn't be making love today. Probably not tomorrow either...

Hell.

"Girls, it's time to go," Callie said, sending him a you-can't-fool-me look. No matter how old they were or how independent, when Callie used that tone of voice, they all made haste to obey.

Jules and Darby rose and they both, as they always did, dropped a kiss on his cheek. Callie, surprisingly, ignored him to wrap her arms around Tanna, who still had her back to them. Levi saw Callie's squeeze and wondered what his mom whispered into her ear.

Sometimes, back then, he'd arrive at the hospital and find Callie lying next to Tanna in her hospital bed, Tanna's head on Callie's shoulder, talking or watching a movie. His mom and Tanna had become close very quickly, and he'd been a little jealous at their easy camaraderie. His relationship with his mom had been collateral damage in his ongoing fights with his dad; she'd been caught in the middle, her loyalty torn in two.

Levi's warnings, his doom-and-gloom prophecies about Ray's risk-taking, had caused tension and a hundred arguments, and then Ray died. Levi was still the only person who knew that Ray, at the time of his death, was about to acquire new cell phone technology that he said would revolutionize the industry. He'd handed over personal and business sureties and had been on the point of signing away everything they owned…

The technology, as Levi discovered after the funeral, was a dud. It didn't work.

They would've lost every damn thing they owned had the deal gone through…

And people wondered why Levi liked to be cautious, why he needed to be in control? His father had taught him how dangerous freewheeling could be…

Callie turned away from Tanna and stood in front of him, waiting for him to meet her eyes. He finally did and Callie shook her head, looking a little amused.

"There's nothing to worry about, Mom," Levi told her, hoping she'd believe him, that he'd start to believe himself.

Her mouth tipped upward at the corners. "Oh, I know there isn't." She bent down and dropped a kiss on his forehead. "I'm not worried at all. Are you?"

Hell no. Even if he was, he'd never admit it to the Grand Interrogator.

Callie's smiled broadened at his negative response. "But I do know that, from tonight on, my darling, your life is never going to be the same again. And I, for one, am thrilled."

Levi watched her walk across the room and resisted the urge to call her back, to try to convince her that she was letting her imagination run wild. That she was seeing stuff that simply wasn't there.

He wanted to explain that he and Tanna were just two people who no longer had anything in common other than their mutual wish to strip each other down and put their hands and tongues to work.

But there were some things you couldn't say to your mom, even if she was one of the coolest people you knew.

"Bye, Mom."

Callie, and her great smile, walked out.

Tanna dropped the pizza crust onto her plate and wiped her fingers on a napkin, thinking it was going to be a very long six weeks if she and Levi couldn't get past their awkward silence.

She took a sip of red wine and tucked her feet under her bottom.

Levi sat in his easy chair, his busted leg resting on a leather ottoman, his hand wrapped around a glass of water and his expression pensive.

"I went to Murphy's today," Tanna said and watched as his eyes flew up to meet hers.

"Yeah?"

His expression was interested so Tanna nodded. "When I left Carrick's office, I couldn't resist popping into the viewing rooms. They are holding a vintage dress and accessories auction soon and the items on display are amazing, one-of-a-kind pieces from some of the most iconic designers of the past. And they are also auctioning off a collection of Henry Moore's work, so I spent some time in the viewing room."

Levi pulled a face. "Remind me who Moore is?"

Levi still wasn't an art connoisseur. "Twentieth-century sculptor? English, best known for his huge bronze sculptures. He dabbled in abstractions of the human figure, often depicting mother-and-child figures. He was a little obsessed with the female body—"

"Aren't we all?" Levi murmured. Okay, she wasn't touching that comment with a ten-foot pole.

"—and his forms often contain hollow spaces," Tanna continued.

"Thank you, Wikipedia," Levi stated, his voice dry.

As she always had before, she provided far too much information when Levi asked her about art. She couldn't help it; art facts stuck in her head like lint stuck to Velcro. She adored art and loved to share her knowledge.

"Did you ever finish your degree in art history?" Levi asked her, his index fingers tapping his strong thigh.

Tanna shook her head. "I got…distracted."

"But I bet your bedside table is still stacked with art books."

Tanna smiled at his observation. It was. Her bedtime reading was catalogues raisonnés and autobiographies of artists.

"It's the first time I've been back to the business since I left when I was nineteen," Tanna said softly, thinking about her visit to Murphy's. She felt Levi's eyes on her face and wondered why she felt the need to tell him something so personal.

Levi put his plate down on the table next to him and tipped his head to the side. "Really? Why haven't you been back?"

Tanna looked down into her glass, gently swirling the liquid so it stuck to the sides of the crystal. How could she explain this? Should she even try?

"Tanna?"

She wrinkled her nose and met his inquisitive gaze. "I've only been back to Boston a handful of times and I didn't want to go back to Murphy's because I was scared it would be too hard. And that I would question my choices about my education and my career."

"And did you?"

She sent him a small smile. She wasn't ready to admit to Levi that it had been hard, a little.

"I watched this woman walk up the stairs. She was wearing an amazing pair of red heels and I followed her up. She was talking to a client about a Schiaparelli dress—"

"English, Murphy."

"Elsa Schiaparelli was an iconic Italian designer. Coco Chanel was her greatest rival, and she was big between the two world wars. She was influenced by surrealists like Salvador Dalí."

Levi groaned and Tanna knew she'd provided too much information again. "Anyway, this woman was talking about this vintage dress and doing a really poor job of selling it. I wanted to rip the phone from her and take over the conversation."

"I presume you managed to restrain yourself?" Levi asked, amused.

Tanna pulled a face. "Barely. She wasn't enthusiastic about the product, didn't respect the process. You've got to have a passion for the product if you're going to sell it effectively, Levi."

"You aren't short of passion, Tanna."

Tanna ignored the obvious double entendre. "Maybe, but that's not my field anymore, Levi. It was something else I gave up when I left."

"It was your choice to walk away, Tanna. That's on you," Levi said, dousing her with a hard dose of reality.

Of course it was, but surely she was allowed to reflect on what she'd given up? She could've had a career at Murphy's; she could've married Levi, be living in this house and having a totally different life. Surely it was normal to wonder what it would be like working with her brothers, indulging her deep love of art, textiles and ceramics, and sharing her passion with collectors?

She could see herself leaving Levi's bed, maybe after some fun in the shower, kissing him goodbye as she left this beautiful house, driving into Boston central. She'd have her own office at Murphy's and she'd spend her time working with the PR department, promoting upcoming sales and meeting with collectors all over the world. She'd travel internationally, visiting clients in Hong Kong and New York, Paris and Dubai. If she had time, she'd visit the Louvre or the Met, the antiques shops and the art dealers.

Pop into a perfumery in Paris, a spice market in Delhi, a boutique on Rodeo Drive.

But she'd always come home to Levi…

Tanna yanked herself out of the daydream, distraught over how real it felt, how natural. In the daydream, she wasn't nineteen, she was the age she was now.

But it wasn't possible and it certainly wasn't real…

Her imagination, sparked by her visit to Murphy's, was just working overtime, playing tricks on her.

So why did it feel more—she searched for the word—*normal* than her current London-based life?

Ridiculous!

She needed to pull herself together, to remind herself what was important. Working at Murphy's had been her dream, her destiny, but everything changed when she put Addy behind the wheel of her car and handed her a death sentence. By giving Addy the keys, Tanna set in motion a train of events that not only led to Addy's death, but also Isla's lifetime of mourning and Tanna walking away from everything she thought she deserved.

And Levi had been collateral damage.

Boston wasn't her city and this wasn't her life anymore. She'd taken a step out of time, that was all. She could only do what she could today, here and now, and that meant clearing her debt to Levi and sorting out her PTSD so she could return to London and her job.

That was real life. This wasn't.

Standing up, Tanna placed her glass of wine on the side table and gave Levi a tight smile. "I'm turning in."

"You're upset." Levi frowned at her, obviously confused. "It couldn't be anything I said because you hardly gave me a chance to speak."

Tanna nodded, taking his point. "It's me, not you, Brogan. Just as always."

Tanna walked out of the room and ran up the stairs, desperately trying to outrun the past.

Six

They made it to the end of the third day by gritting their teeth and trying, really hard, to be polite. But on Wednesday afternoon, Tanna left Levi's house mid-afternoon, telling him she'd be back shortly, but it was two hours before he heard her footsteps on his wooden floor. Two hours, ten minutes and fifty-three seconds.

Not that he was counting.

Sitting in his father's old wingback, his leg propped up on an ottoman, his heart kicked up a beat when he saw her standing in the doorway, holding a shopping bag in her right hand.

"Where have you been?" he demanded.

Tanna raised her eyebrows at his tone and it took all he had not to apologize.

She was here to help him and they had a deal. She

was paying off a debt. This was about a little light revenge.

But that didn't mean he had to act like a jerk.

"Sorry." Levi ran his hand over his face before moving his eyes back to her lovely face. "What's in the bag, Tanna?" he asked her, feeling infinitely weary.

"Give me ten minutes and I'll show you."

Before he could question her further, she disappeared into the house and Levi wished he could follow her out the door but moving quickly wasn't a skill he currently possessed. He swallowed down a surge of panic at being confined and, very deliberately, breathed deeply.

Suck it up, cupcake.

"Levi?"

Levi lifted his head at Tanna's call. "Yeah?" he responded, raising his voice.

"Come here."

Levi hobbled to the doorway, walked down the long hall and caught his breath outside the half-closed door to the small bathroom at the end. He pushed the door open with the tip of his crutch and was rewarded with an amazing view of Tanna bent over the bath, her perfect ass in the air.

Levi's cargo shorts tightened as his cock told him, in the only way it knew, how much it appreciated the view. Levi wanted to grip those slim legs, explore the soft skin of her inner thighs, see if his hands could encircle her tiny waist. He wanted to twist her long hair around his hands, plunder her mouth.

He wanted Tanna more than he wanted the use of his

leg back, and since he was comprehensively frustrated at his lack of mobility, that was saying something.

"The reason I am here?"

Tanna sat back on her heels, pushed a silky curl the color of midnight off her cheek and turned her head to look at him. She gestured to the bathtub. "I thought you might want a shower."

He'd freakin' kill for a shower but that wasn't going to happen since he couldn't get his cast wet.

"I'm an accident waiting to happen, Tanna," Levi brusquely told her, hating, as always, to admit weakness.

"That was when you didn't have me." Tanna gracefully climbed to her feet and when she stepped away, he saw two stools in the bathtub and a handheld shower attachment. For the first time in days, possibly since his accident, his mouth turned up in a genuine smile. This could work.

Except…

"I can't get my cast wet. And plastic bags don't work."

Tanna picked up a long plastic sleeve and a roll of duct tape. "This is a cast cover and—" she held up the roll of tape "—this is waterproof tape. I guarantee the cast will stay dry. Strip off and I'll help you into the bath."

Yeah, no. Because, while he was a guy who had a lot of control—a man who prided himself on it—this was Tanna, the girl he'd never had and always wanted. The woman who haunted his dreams. And if he stripped down, she'd see how much she affected him and that wasn't acceptable.

"Problem?" Tanna asked him.

"I'll shower but I'll keep my shorts on."

Tanna rolled her eyes. "I have seen naked men before, Brogan. I'm pretty sure you have the same bits they have."

A red mist danced across Levi's eyes at the thought of Tanna being naked with another man, her hands on his body, her mouth on someone else's... *No, can't go there.*

Not ever going there.

Tanna placed her hands on her hips and her gaze ping-ponged between him and the tub. "So, are you going to do this or not?"

Hell yes, he was going to shower. And he'd deal with the embarrassment factor when it came up. And it would come up. Levi hobbled into the bathroom and wished they were in his newly renovated master bathroom upstairs. In that ample space, he could have put some distance between himself and Tanna; they'd have room to breathe. But this bathroom was minuscule, and he could smell her perfume, feel her heat, see her pulse beating in the cord of her neck.

So, she wasn't as unaffected by him as she liked to pretend. Good to know.

Levi placed his crutches between the commode and the basin and pulled his T-shirt up his chest, catching the appreciation on Tanna's face as she looked at his body. He worked hard to stay in shape and seeing her desire made all those long gym sessions worth it.

Keeping his hands off his onetime fiancée while he got naked was going to be damn difficult.

"Let's get this plastic cover on," Tanna said, her voice sounding brisk.

Before he could protest, Tanna dropped to her haunches and started to slide the cover over his toes and up his shin. Her hands moved up and under his shorts and he silently implored her to go a little higher, to cover his balls, to stroke his...

Get a grip, Brogan.

"Hold the plastic in place, please," Tanna said, her voice husky. She had to be aware of the effect she was having on him, his cock was a steel rod tenting his pants. He didn't reply, mostly because his brain didn't have enough blood to power his mouth.

"I'm going to tape it down." Tanna looked up at him, her green eyes large and compelling. This was how she'd look if she was actually going down on him.

Holy crap.

"Do you want me to shave your leg?"

Okay, what? "Why?" He croaked the one-word question.

"It's going to hurt when we take the tape off unless I shave your hair."

Not happening. Not in this lifetime. "I have a busted patella. I can handle a little hair pulling."

Tanna's mouth twitched. "So says every man who thinks he can endure a wax. Okay, your call."

Tanna taped the plastic to his thigh and rested on her heels, pushing her hair back with her wrist. "Sit down on the edge of the tub and let's get your shorts off."

Not wanting to shock her, Levi reached for a wash-cloth before sitting down. He flipped the button of his shorts open, undid the zip and pushed the washcloth under the fabric, hoping it would keep him moderately decent.

Tanna arched her eyebrows. "Don't bother on my account."

His hand stilled, and their eyes clashed, and Levi saw the passion in those green depths. And curiosity.

To hell with it. He pulled the washcloth out, tossed it away and met her gaze with defiance. "I was trying to be polite."

"You've never been polite in your life," Tanna scoffed. "And you have a beautiful body. You shouldn't be ashamed of it."

"I'm not ashamed of my body," Levi retorted, annoyed.

"And you shouldn't be," Tanna told him, sounding patronizing.

Annoyed by her cool tone, Levi gripped her chin with his fingers. "I have a hard-on from hell. I was covering it up."

Tanna's tongue flicked out to touch her top lip. "I noticed," she replied, her voice husky.

"It wants what it never had."

"I figured that out too."

He couldn't help it; he needed to taste her. He needed to know whether her mouth was as warm as he remembered from their first kiss, whether she could still make his head swim.

Levi curled his fingers into the band of her jeans

and tugged her to stand between his legs. He rested his forehead between her breasts, trying to calm his breathing. This was a bad idea. Once they went down this slippery slope, they wouldn't be able to stop the ride. Kissing her, fully clothed, was one thing. His being half-naked was a lot more dangerous.

"I want you, Tanna," he growled, resisting the urge to pull one of those nipples pushing against the fabric of her shirt.

Tanna didn't reply but her hand stroked the side of his neck, pushed into his hair.

"I don't want to want you. I'm over you," Levi informed her, wondering whether he was trying to convince her or himself.

Levi lifted his head and his eyes clashed with hers, deep blue smacking into her green. Tanna nodded. "Got it. But…just one taste," Tanna murmured, bending down to brush her lips across his. But instead of taking it deeper, Tanna made a gentle exploration of his mouth and Levi relished the getting-to-know-you-again kiss.

It was simple and sexy and…yeah, sweet.

Then Tanna slipped her tongue past his teeth to tangle with his and Levi waited for the bathroom to catch alight, for the walls to blow apart. Fireworks danced across his skin as they fought for dominance of the kiss, both taking and demanding and giving and feeding…

Levi banded his arm around her butt. This was all that was important; feasting on Tanna was all he needed. As long as she was kissing him, he could forget everything else.

Levi heard her mutter his name against his lips and thought he'd never liked the way it sounded until now. He wanted to hear it as he stripped her down, his lips on her breast, on her stomach, tasting the sweet honey between her thighs.

He needed her to yell his name as she shattered on his tongue and again when he pushed inside her...

"Okay, this can't happen."

It took Levi a few moments to make sense of the words, to realize her hands on his shoulders were trying to put some space between them. He licked his lips and looked at her, disconcerted. Why was she stopping?

Tanna pushed her hair back as his hands dropped from her body. She took a step back, then another, and he could hear her ragged breathing in the small room.

Or was that his breathing? Who knew?

"You need to shower, and I know you are in pain."

Well, yeah. But they could still have some fun.

"Wrong time, wrong place."

Her suggestion was sensible, but he didn't want to be freakin' sensible. He wanted to be naked, with Tanna wrapped around him.

Levi placed his hands on her hips and drew circles on her hip bones. "Bend down so I can kiss you again."

Tanna slapped his hands away. "Brogan! Concentrate!"

The moment, it seemed, had passed. *Dammit*.

"Right, let's concentrate on getting you into the tub,"

Tanna said, sounding remarkably brisk and nurse-like. And, because he was a guy, the image of Tanna dressed in a tiny, revealing nurse outfit—displaying a deep cleavage, wearing fishnet stockings and red heels— flashed on his retinas. Levi groaned and tipped his head back to look at the ceiling.

Since he wasn't about to get lucky, he'd take a shower.

Levi, with Tanna's help, got his pants off and they both ignored his erection. Well, as much as they could ignore a hard-as-hell, wanting-to-play cock.

Levi swung his legs over the side of the tub and set- tled himself on the stool. Tanna helped lift his injured leg onto the other stool and quickly and efficiently placed soap, a loofah and shampoo in easy reach. She tossed the washcloth and it landed on his crotch, which wasn't, he was sure, a mistake.

Tanna flipped open the taps and hot water hit his shoulders as she gave him the handheld showerhead.

Levi directed the hot water at his face, at his neck. God, it felt amazing. But not nearly as good as kiss- ing Tanna had.

"Call me when you are done," Tanna said, walking toward the door.

Levi opened his eyes and called her back. When she turned, he saw confusion in her eyes and, beneath it, still-bubbling desire.

"Thank you for doing this. For thinking of this. I was so tired of washing up in the basin."

Tanna handed him a soft smile, flipping his heart

inside out. She nodded before walking through the door and closing it behind her.

Levi dropped the showerhead and looked down at his still hard erection. He could, easily, take care of the problem, but he didn't want to do it solo.

He wanted female hands, a feminine mouth, a gentle touch.

He only wanted Tanna…

Dammit.

Tanna heard Levi's crutches hitting the wooden floor and shook her head. She'd left clean underwear, shorts and a T-shirt on the bathroom cabinet earlier but she'd expected him to call for her to help him out of the tub.

But the man was too damn stubborn to ask for help.

Levi shuffled into the kitchen and Tanna cast an eye over his body, appreciating his wide, muscled chest, the light body hair narrowing into a thin line bisecting a muscled stomach and disappearing beneath the band of his shorts. He held the black T-shirt in his hands and his leg still sported the plastic cast cover.

He was battered and a little dented but, God, he was gorgeous. Masculine, sexy, big and bold. Tanna felt warm as she recalled his big hands on her butt, his tongue in her mouth, demanding more, wanting everything.

Levi wouldn't be a gentle lover—oh, he'd never hurt her, but he'd demand everything from her. He'd wring every drop of pleasure from her. In his arms, she knew, she might find herself, sexually.

And, she was pretty sure, he'd be the one to finally—finally—give her the orgasm she'd never experienced from a man's touch.

But sleeping with Levi was a bad idea. A terrible idea. Because if it was as good as his kisses suggested it would be, it would make leaving him, leaving Boston, hard. She had a career to salvage, people to save, her PTSD symptoms to conquer. She had a bigger debt to repay than the one she owed Levi.

She couldn't afford to be distracted by the still-gorgeous Levi Brogan.

She would *not* be distracted…

Tanna pushed her hair off her shoulders and reminded herself Levi didn't want anything from her…

Nothing but sex.

Strangely, and very irrationally considering her need to leave Boston, the thought made her sad.

Levi stopped at the chair next to the big, well-used kitchen table. Gorgeous skin, dotted with freckles and covering bulging, rippling muscles—Tanna swallowed, looking for the smallest hint of moisture in her mouth.

Nope, nothing.

Tanna looked at the dish towel in her hands and remembered a time when it had felt natural to step up to him, to place her mouth on his.

Levi cleared his throat and Tanna jumped, embarrassment coloring her face. Refusing to meet his eyes, she knew he'd be wearing a know-it-all smirk. She looked down at the floor, and when she raised her head again, Levi was dressed.

"Feel free to take it off again if you like," Levi suggested, gesturing to his shirt.

Annoyed by his smirk, by his complete faith that she was crazy attracted to him—she was but he didn't need to rub it in her face!—Tanna felt the need to do something to remind him who he was messing with...

She wasn't nineteen anymore and desperately eager to please...

Without giving Levi any warning, Tanna caught the corner of the piece of tape on his thigh and yanked it super hard. Levi yelped as the tape separated hair from his skin and he immediately gripped his leg, stopping her from pulling the rest of the tape away.

"What the hell are you doing?" Levi demanded, his eyes glistening.

She couldn't help teasing him. "I thought you said you could handle a little waxing."

"I was wrong. So, so wrong," Levi told her, his hands not moving from his leg.

Tanna laughed. "Stop being a baby. Millions of women, me included, do this on a regular basis."

"There are these things called razors," Levi grumbled.

"I offered, remember?" Tanna peeled his fingers away from the plaster cast. "The only way to get this off is to go hard and go fast. I'm going to count to three and then rip it away, okay?"

Levi nodded, locked his teeth and Tanna held the tape tightly. "Okay, here we go... One."

Tanna ripped the tape, and Levi gasped, and the

plastic sleeve fell down his thigh. Tanna stood up, clapped her hands together and grinned. "Done!"

"You are truly evil," Levi told her. "What happened to counting to three?"

Tanna shrugged. "Lightweight."

Tanna tossed the tape, folded the plastic sleeve and washed her hands. Then she walked over to the counter and picked up the vine tomatoes she'd been slicing and tossed them into a skillet on the gas stove. The insanely good combination of basil, garlic, tomatoes and olive oil filled the room.

"What are you making?"

"Pasta and vegetables in a tomato sauce," Tanna replied, leaving the stove to look for spices.

Levi looked disappointed. "Please tell me there's protein in there, somewhere."

"Chicken breasts are baking in the oven."

"There is a God," Levi murmured, pulling his shirt halfway up his chest to scratch a spot just under his ribs. Tanna noticed his ripped stomach, that fine happy trail and his warm, tanned skin.

"You okay?" Levi asked her, dropping his shirt, and Tanna nearly whimpered her disappointment.

No, I want sex. With you. Now.

I'll even go on top...

"Fine."

Liar, liar, thong on fire. Tanna walked back to the stove, stirring the contents of her pan. Needing wine, and to cool down, she opened the fridge and jammed her head inside.

"How was your shower?" Tanna asked, pulling out

a bottle of merlot. She also took out a jug of iced tea and poured Levi a glass.

Levi's smiled flashed and Tanna was sure the earth sighed in appreciation. "It was amazing. It's so nice to feel properly clean."

"So, is dirt bike riding a new thing?" Tanna asked, tossing the pasta into a pot of boiling water.

"Within the last eighteen months or so," Levi replied. "Finn introduced me to the sport." Levi winced and pulled a face. "Uh, you do know Finn is a bit of adrenaline junkie?"

Tanna shrugged. "I do. I've told him I will kill him if he hurts himself doing something stupid."

His smile tilted the world off its axis again. Tanna tipped her head to look at him. There were fine lines at the corners of his twinkling eyes and his lips stretched into a we-can-melt-steel smile.

Hot. So hot.

"You should smile more often. You've got a great smile," Tanna said, her words falling into the silence of the kitchen.

Tanna felt the urge to backtrack, to tell him she didn't think their sleeping together sometime in the immediate future was a good idea. Because, oh, too many things...

He was too much, too masculine, too attractive, too able to make her feel things she couldn't, or didn't want to, deal with. He made her want, and worst of all, he made her question.

Her past. Her present. And her future.

"Sauce is burning, Murphy."

Levi's prosaic statement cut through her panic and Tanna whirled around to see smoke coming off the pan. Cursing, she quickly stirred the sauce, relieved she'd caught it in time.

Now, if she could save herself from falling under Brogan's spell again, that would be an even better result.

Seven

Tanna topped off her coffee cup and, glancing over her shoulder, saw Levi's attention was still on the screen of his laptop. Rimless wire glasses made his blue eyes seem darker, look more serious and older than his years. A frown pulled his strong eyebrows together and she smiled as he lobbed quiet insults at his state-of-the-art machine.

After picking up her coffee, she leaned her butt against the marble counter. "Problem?"

Levi lifted his head to look at her. "Payroll, company accounts."

"For the marina?" She knew Levi owned a majority share in a marina downtown with Noah Lockwood and she recalled one of her brothers telling her he'd revamped the business so it was one of the best, and most technologically advanced, marinas on the East Coast.

"And for the boatyard, and my other two marinas."

So, how to ask this without causing offense? Everyone knew Ray left the family billions, that neither Levi, Callie nor his sisters needed to work if they didn't want to. Hell, she was pretty sure their kids and grandkids wouldn't need to work either.

"Um, I didn't think you were so hands-on. I thought you had people to take care of the day-to-day stuff."

"I do have people who are very capable at running my businesses but I'm a control freak, hadn't you noticed? I don't hand over control easily and I like to know what's happening, every day."

"I definitely remember the control freak aspect of your personality. I remember you having very definite ideas about what you wanted for our wedding."

Not meaning to rake up the past and the unpleasantness that went along with it, she waved her comment away. "But I didn't know you owned so many businesses."

Levi lifted his uninjured shoulder. "I have a few but it's a fraction of what my father owned."

Judging by his flat, offhand comment, Tanna knew there was a story behind his hard statement. "Do you *want* to own as many businesses as your dad?" she carefully asked.

Levi released an irritated sigh and leaned back in his chair. "My father was a multibillionaire, one of the most successful businessmen in the state. I have a long way to go before I hit such illustrious heights."

He hadn't answered her question and his tone oozed sarcasm. She still didn't understand his subtext. "But do you want to be as successful as him?"

"I'm the son, his heir. He expected it. The world expects it."

Again, an answer that wasn't an answer. "But is that what you *want*?"

Levi glared at her, and without replying, returned to his screen. Okay, so that was his tender spot. She wondered if he had others.

She'd only met Levi's father a few times after their engagement and she remembered a charming man, with a personality as big as the sun. He walked into the room and immediately dominated it with his loud voice, his raucous laughter and his inimitable charm. His light shone bright and Tanna distinctly remembered Levi's mental withdrawal with every passing minute they spent with his dad.

The louder Ray got, the quieter Levi became.

Levi wasn't naturally ebullient; he was, fundamentally, reticent and reserved. Ray had tossed question after question at her, asking her about her accident, her family, how it felt to lose her parents at a young age, whether she thought her brothers had done a good job raising her. Ray didn't have any boundaries and no tact and she'd been grateful when Levi, with a few words quietly uttered, had shut down the interrogation.

At the time she'd been grateful Levi removed the spotlight from her and had gone on to enjoy her lunch. Now, with a little maturity and hindsight, she could look back on that lunch and see that Levi spoke and Ray had listened. And obeyed.

Tanna wondered if Levi knew how much his father had respected him…

"Tell me about your relationship with your dad," Tanna said after blowing air across the surface of her hot coffee.

"Trying to work here, Murphy," Levi retorted and stared at his screen. After a minute, he threw down his pen and leaned back in his chair, his red Henley pulling tight across his biceps as he folded his arms across his wide chest.

Classic defensive pose, Brogan. What are you hiding?

"He was my dad. What's there to say?"

Behind those glasses there was so much pain in his eyes, and a whole lot of unresolved emotion. And, because this was Levi, it was all covered by a solid layer of don't-go-there.

"I liked your dad. He was charming. A bit over the top but, yeah, charismatic," Tanna quietly told him. "But he wouldn't be the person I ran to in a crisis."

Levi linked his hands behind his head, looking interested. "Why do you say that?"

Tanna lifted one shoulder. "Because I sensed that, in geology terms, Callie was the rock, the foundation of your family. Ray, to me, was the pretty streaks of gold or the flash of quartz, the trace of platinum. He provided the flash while Callie provided the stability."

Levi sent her a hard stare before releasing a long, steady sigh. "Wow. That's pretty astute of you."

Tanna half smiled at him. "You want to know what else I think?"

She could see the doubt in his eyes, and wondered whether he'd change the subject, push their conversation in another direction. Years ago, Levi always, always avoided emotional discussions.

He surprised her when he gestured for her to continue. "I think you made your dad feel uncomfortable…"

Levi jerked back, shocked. "That's not possible, Tanna."

"I'm sure you did. I think your dad saw something in you he didn't have."

"And what would that be?"

Tanna tapped the side of her mug with her finger. "When he said something controversial, he looked at you, needing to see your reaction. It was like he was looking for your approval."

Levi shook his head. "Nope, my dad never listened to anything I had to say, especially in business. If I said black, he said white."

Maybe that was because Levi always seemed so happy in his skin, so totally and utterly in control. Little rattled him and maybe Ray, who commanded attention from everybody else, wanted his son's attention more than anyone else's.

"I think he wanted you to be proud of him."

Levi rolled his eyes. "If he wanted that, he shouldn't have taken such enormous risks, shouldn't have gambled every cent he owned on crazy propositions."

Surely Levi couldn't hold that against him? "Your father made billions doing that, Levi."

"Luckily they panned out. Possibly, I think, because God looks after the stupid." Levi rested his arms on the kitchen table, his frown pulling his strong eyebrows together, blue eyes troubled.

"Everybody sees him as being this incredible businessman and he was, to a point. But he got lucky more often than he should've. There were times, during some of his biggest deals, when I was on the edge of my seat, waiting to hear if we'd lost everything."

They'd had a lot to lose. "You would've still had this house, the cars, personal bank accounts."

Levi's smile was cold. "You don't understand, Tanna. On *all* of his deals he risked *everything*. He put everything on the line to raise the cash he needed— this house, all the houses, the investments, our college funds. Everything got tossed into the pot."

"Wow. That bad, huh?"

"That bad," Levi confirmed. "That's why I stopped working for him. I couldn't make him see reason and I couldn't control his wild impulses. He was gambling with the company and I could see it going south. I needed to get out and start up something new, so we'd have a source of income when we lost everything."

Tanna winced. "You were sure that was going to happen?"

"Oh, hell yes. Absolutely positive. When he died…" Levi stopped talking, cursed and waved his words away.

Tanna cursed too when he didn't continue his explanation, wishing he trusted her enough to complete his sentence.

When he returned his attention to his laptop, Tanna continued to stare at him, her mind whirling.

"So, that's why you like to be in control, why you like your ducks in a row. Because your father's ducks were drunk and at a rave."

Levi lifted his head, frowning until he made sense of her words. Then he smiled. "I suppose that's a good way to describe him. My dad thrived on chaos. I do not."

Tanna returned to her earlier thought, that Ray wanted approval from his son. "Maybe he wanted to impress you and he kept doing that by launching into bigger and riskier deals. Maybe he wanted to show you he could do it."

Levi sighed. "Then he didn't know me at all. I'm not impressed by flash."

"Maybe that was all he knew how to be," Tanna murmured. This was the first time Levi had ever said something this personal, had cracked the door to what went on behind his implacable facade. She wanted to know more, she wanted to know everything.

So when she heard the sharp rap on the kitchen door, she nearly howled in frustration. Tanna darted a look at Levi and he, not surprisingly, looked like a French aristocrat who'd been spared a meeting with Madame Guillotine.

The kitchen door opened and Tanna smiled as Carrick walked in, closely followed by the stunning blonde she'd met at Carrick's offices.

After giving her a quick hug, Carrick gestured to the blonde. "Meet Sadie. She's working with us to authenticate what we think might be a lost Winslow Homer. Levi Brogan and my sister, Tanna."

Tanna sent Carrick an exasperated look. "You introduced Sadie to me at Murphy's, Carrick. Don't you remember?"

Probably not since she was convinced his blood had left his brain on seeing the sexy PhD.

Tanna watched Levi's reaction as Sadie walked over to him to shake his hand. Tanna waited for the flash of attraction in his eyes, the slow smile she knew could melt panties at fifty paces.

Well, huh. Nothing, zip, diddly-squat. They shook hands, exchanged polite smiles and she didn't even pick up a hint of zing. They were two spectacular-looking humans. How could they *not* be attracted to each other?

Tanna turned her attention to Carrick and, yep, there she saw what she'd been looking for in Levi's reaction to Sadie. Carrick's green eyes, so much like hers, flickered with possession, a hint of jealousy and a healthy dose of irritation. The latter was probably directed at himself for allowing himself to be distracted by the gorgeous blonde.

Well, well, well…this could be interesting.

"Did you come to see me, or Levi?" Tanna asked Carrick.

She was his sister but Levi was his best friend.

"Both of you."

Tanna gestured to the empty seats at the table. "Can I get you coffee?" They both nodded, shed their coats and took seats next to and opposite Levi, who closed the lid of his laptop. Levi asked Sadie about her career as an art detective and they were soon engaged in a lively conversation about Sadie's attempts to track down the painting's provenance.

It all sounded wonderful, and interesting.

"You should document the process, Carrick. Show your clients how you go about authenticating a work of art. They'd be interested, I'm sure. You could do it as a series of vlogs." Tanna grinned. "It helps you are both pretty."

Carrick sent her a penetrating stare. "That's a really good idea. I'll run it by the owners of the painting and the PR department." He tipped his head to the side. "When are you going to come and head up our PR department?"

Tanna pretended to think about it. "Uh…never?"

"Damn." Carrick pulled a face. "Talking of PR, I came up with an idea of my own I'd like your help with. It's why I'm here, actually."

Now that sounded intriguing. Tanna, coffee forgotten, gave him her full attention. "I'm listening."

"Next Friday night, Murphy's is hosting a cocktail party to promote next week's sale of, mostly, vintage haute couture and high-end fashion. We have jewelry, accessories and, obviously, some of the once-in-a-lifetime gowns by the most prominent and feted designers of the twentieth century."

"I know. I saw the collection at Murphy's. It's wonderful."

Carrick cleared his throat. "You might not know this, Levi, but Tanna's mom, my stepmom, collected amazing ensembles from the twenties through to the eighties."

"Is Mom's clothing collection part of the sale?" Tanna demanded, horrified. As a child she'd played dress-up with her outfits and when she was sad, mad or needing her mom, she'd often gone into that spacious closet located in the dance studio at the Beacon Hill house to feel closer to her mother.

Carrick shook his head. "Of course not. It doesn't belong to me."

Tanna frowned, confused. As the eldest son, Carrick had inherited the family home and all its contents. When they all became adults and moved into their own places, Carrick had offered to split the contents between the four of them but they all wanted the house to remain the way their parents left it.

"Yes, it does."

Carrick shook his head. "The collection is yours, Tan. She would've wanted you to have it. Besides, I'd look silly wearing a Coco Chanel."

Tanna blinked back her tears, thinking that it had been too long since she'd seen the collection. As soon as she could, she'd go home and see what she owned.

Carrick cleared his throat and adjusted his already perfect tie. "Anyway, we're having a cocktail party to show off the sale collection to a very select handful of collectors and fashion editors and Jane, our head of PR, suggested putting up some photos of Mom dressed in some of her designer gowns. I wanted to run it by you first."

Tanna placed her hand on her chest and sighed. "Aw, I love that. It's such a great idea."

"An even better idea would be for Tanna to wear one of her mom's vintage gowns to the party," Levi suggested.

Tanna's surprise was reflected in Carrick's eyes and on Sadie's face.

"That's a really excellent idea." Carrick quietly agreed.

Levi immediately looked grumpy. "I have them occasionally." He pushed his hand through his hair and rubbed the back of his neck before continuing. "Tanna looks a lot like Raeni and if she changed a few times during the cocktail party, showing off different gowns, she would, together with her mom's photos wearing the same gowns, make a hell of an impact."

Carrick smiled at his friend. "Want to come and head up my PR department since my sister won't?"

Levi looked horrified. "I'd rather shoot myself in my already injured foot."

Carrick grinned at his sarcastic reply and looked at Tanna. "What do you say, Tan?"

He was asking her to wear her mom's stunning gowns and her amazing jewelry, drink champagne, and talk art and fashion with some of the best minds in the business? Oh, yeah, she was so in.

Attending the event didn't mean this was her life anymore. It was just one night of pleasure. Surely she was entitled to a little fun before returning to London?

It would be a night to remember. "Sure."

"Excellent. I'll get Jane to email you Mom's photos

and you can choose the gowns you want to wear." Carrick stood up and pulled out Sadie's chair as she rose with him. "We don't have time to get anything altered so keep that in mind."

Tanna nodded. "I'll liaise with Jane and we'll get it sorted."

Carrick, his hand on Sadie's back—interesting—bent his head to kiss Tanna's cheek. "Thanks, Tan. Later, Levi."

"Later," Levi replied, flipping open the lid to his computer.

"Don't kill each other," Carrick told them as he ushered Sadie out the back door.

Tanna grinned. "We'll try."

At the marina, Levi settled himself into the passenger seat and glowered through the windscreen as Tanna pulled into traffic, heading for Carrick's house in Beacon Hill.

He hated not being able to drive his own vehicle, Levi decided. Handing over control, even something as simple as driving, annoyed him. Levi felt relieved when Tanna pulled up to her magnificent childhood house in Beacon Hill and parked his luxury Lexus SUV under the magnolia tree. He'd been concerned about how she'd handle his super-expensive car, but she hadn't seemed intimidated and she handled the large vehicle like a pro.

After Carrick and Sadie left, Tanna told him she had a two-hour appointment in the city and her closed-off expression suggested he not ask any further questions, which, honestly, just made him want to know who she was meeting and why she wanted to keep it a secret. Her reticence intrigued him; the Tanna he used to know couldn't keep a secret to save her life.

But Tanna was no longer the girl he'd loved. She was now a fully independent woman who marched to the beat of her own drum. He'd adored his fiancée but this version of Tanna was, in many ways, even more intriguing. Tanna-today had an edge to her he found exciting and whenever he thought he had her pegged, she moved the goalposts and kept him guessing. Tanna-today was exciting, mysterious and more than a little addictive.

Levi—understanding she wouldn't share any personal information with him until she was good and ready to do so, which might be never—had asked her, since she was headed in the same direction, to drive him to the marina so he could touch base with his staff and see how his business was faring in his absence.

So, after arranging for Tanna to collect him later, he'd spent an hour in his office with his manager before taking a tour of the marina.

He was paying for his physical activity now, but he couldn't regret his actions. He wasn't a rule-from-the-office boss. He liked to get down and dirty, and he worked the business from the ground up. He greeted his staff, approved some requisitions and checked on his maintenance crew. Levi was very aware winter brought many problems to the marina; with the recent winter storms, he was worried his staff wasn't monitoring the snow loads, especially on the finger piers. The weight of the snow could push the piers under the water, taking the electrical connections with them.

It had happened before, and it wasn't a scenario he ever wanted to repeat. Winter at the marina was quiet but it was also a never-ending ball ache. And that was without him being incapacitated.

But his staff had everything under control and he hadn't been needed. The thought both pleased and terrified him.

"Are you sure I can't take you home?" Tanna asked.

"Stop fussing, Tan," Levi told her and he heard the irritation in his voice. "I know you are itching to look at your mom's collection of dresses. We can order lunch. From previous visits to Carrick's house, I know that there's an awesome Chinese place around the corner and they will deliver."

He'd been watching her eyes earlier when he made the suggestion about her wearing her mom's clothing— where the burst of inspiration came from, he had no idea—and quickly realized he'd never seen such a spark of excitement in her eyes, that particular expression on her face.

It was part sadness, part delight, all enthusiasm.

He wasn't sure if she was eager about wearing her mom's clothes, or the exhibition, or thrilled to be involved in Murphy International's business again.

In the hospital, all those years ago, she'd spoken about the PR role her mom played in the business and often told him that when she graduated with her degree in art history, she wanted to follow in her mom's footsteps.

Her mom had been a PR wizard and it was her hard work that made Murphy's one of the most prominent and visible auction houses in the country.

But then Tanna left and took a completely different path, forging another career in emergency medicine. A career she didn't talk about much. Or at all.

Tanna pushed her sunglasses onto the top of her head, pulling back her black curls to reveal her beautiful face. "I really do want to look at her clothes. I've been racking my brain trying to remember what the collection contains since it's been over twelve years since I last saw it."

Tanna stared at the oversize black front door in front of her. "I used to go and hide out in her closet when I was a kid."

Levi nodded. "You probably scuttled in there when times got tough, when you needed a connection to your mom. When you needed *a* mom."

Tanna turned to face him, surprised. "How do you know that?"

Because he knew her, just as she knew him. Despite spending so much time apart, they were still, somehow, in sync. He with her and she with him.

Levi thought back to their earlier conversations and Tanna's reflections about his dad. Her observations had been remarkably astute, and it was funny she easily looked past his dad's charisma to the man beneath. Just like she looked past Levi's reticence and self-sufficiency to find the pieces of himself he kept hidden from the rest of the world.

Seeing Tanna was still waiting for an answer, Levi shrugged. "Good guess."

Not wanting to get into it, Levi opened his door and sighed at the blast of frigid air swirling in through the open door. Tanna took the hint, hopped out of the car and ran around the hood. Opening the door behind him, she pulled his crutches off the back seat and handed them to him before taking a dayglow yellow beanie from her coat pocket and pulling it over her ears.

"Hey, that's my hat!" Levi protested. His favorite, in fact.

"I found it in the laundry basket." Tanna didn't look remotely fazed. "And you don't wear hats."

"I do when I'm skiing."

Tanna cocked her head, her smile a touch smug. "Are you skiing now? Are you going to be skiing soon?"

She had him there. Levi shook his head and jammed his crutches under his armpits. "Were you always this annoying?"

Her laughter cut through the icy winter air. "Oh, I've honed my skills over the years. And, scarily, I'm making a concerted effort to be polite."

God help him.

Eight

Levi settled himself in Carrick's library, grateful to get off his feet. He accepted Tanna's offer of a cup of coffee and after dialing in their lunch order, he pulled out his laptop and booted it up.

He had work to do—specifically, Brogan Family Trust work—and could do it as well here as he could at home. After telling Tanna, for the third time, that he was fine, he asked her to get the door when their lunch arrived before waving her away.

Time passed quickly, the doorbell rang and a minute later he saw Tanna's long, bare legs—her butt barely covered by something looking like a black bandage—as she streaked past the library door.

What the hell was she wearing?

"Tanna!" he bellowed.

Two seconds later she stood in the doorway and Levi snapped his teeth closed so his tongue didn't hit the floor.

She wore the smallest dress he'd ever seen, made from a slinky fabric clinging to her every curve and showing off her finely muscled, long, smooth, tanned legs. Her feet were slender, ending in red-tipped toes. On the inside of her left foot she had a tattoo of a star-burst and a gold ring encompassed the third toe on her right foot.

He forced his eyes up… The dress was comprised of various slits and rips, revealing a large portion of her tanned stomach and most of the right cup of her bright red bra.

"What the hell are you wearing?" he croaked.

Forget getting a little revenge, this woman was going to kill him.

Tanna picked up the tattered hem of the ripped skirt. If he could call the strips a skirt. "It's a grunge dress, from the eighties. I'm not sure who the designer is. I'd have to look that up, but it's exquisitely made."

It was a pile of rags. And it was probably worth a freakin' fortune.

This…this was a great example of why women were so difficult to figure out.

The doorbell rang again and Tanna started to turn. He yelled at her to stop and threw up his hands at her puzzled expression. "You cannot answer the door wear-ing that dress. Do you want to give the delivery guy heart failure?"

Tanna looked down, grimaced and met his eyes. "Dammit. Okay, I'll get changed."

Levi reached for his crutches and hauled himself onto his feet. "I'll get it. You…" He closed his eyes, bemused. Dammit, how could something so…okay, ugly—he wasn't brave enough to say the word out loud—look so good on her?

It was an enigma.

"Go get changed, Tan." *Please, for the love of God, put something decent on before I do something stupid. Like rip that so-called dress off your body…*

Then again, he doubted anyone would notice any damage to the dress, or whatever the hell that thing was.

Tanna left and Levi told his heart to hang in there. Taking a couple of deep breaths, he ambled down the hallway to the magnificent foyer, where a Jackson Pollack dominated the one free wall. Years ago, Carrick had taken him on a tour of the historic house, casually telling him about the Vermeer in the sitting room and the Dalí in the dining room. In one of the reception rooms there was a credenza once owned by the Sun King. It had, apparently, started its life at the palace at Versailles.

And he'd thought his dad was rich. He was, in money and in assets, but in art and collectibles, the Murphys had him beat. Not that it was a competition…

After paying the deliveryman and tipping him well—it was cold and windy and the guy had been cheerful—Levi took the food to the kitchen and walked back into the hall. Calling for Tanna, he was surprised when her voice came from a room two doors down.

On his crutches, Levi walked down the long hallway and stopped at a partially open door. He pushed the door open and saw Tanna standing in front of a mirrored wall in a room holding a ballet barre and a wood parquet dance floor. Floor-to-ceiling mirrors covered three walls. Food forgotten, he stared at her, entranced.

He wasn't a guy who knew a lot about clothes but he had been raised in a house filled with girls so he could, just, describe the gown Tanna wore as a black tulle dress in a series of layers. It was as tame as the previous outfit had been crazy, but this dress, concealing most of Tanna's exquisite body, was sexier, more intriguing.

He stepped into the room and rested his back against the barre, trying to ignore his reflection in so many mirrors. "I think Carrick skipped this room when he took me on the tour all those years ago."

"My mom was an accomplished ballerina. I took lessons all my life and we both used this room to practice," Tanna explained. She gestured to a plain door across the room. "There's the built-in closet, if you want to take a look."

"Yeah, dresses aren't my thing," Levi replied, his tone dry. "I wouldn't know what I'm looking at."

Tanna turned and smiled at him. "Fair enough. To educate you, the dress I'm wearing is a Jean Patou, circa 1930." She stroked the fabric like it was the soft coat of a well-loved cat. "Confession time. I love clothes. I especially love old clothes. I'm a design nut and I love what clothes say about a certain time in history. It's crazy I spend my days in a very practical, very unflattering jumpsuit."

Her eyes clouded over, and she stared off into space for a minute.

Levi wanted to know what was going through her very agile brain. "Tell me about your job."

Tanna lifted the top layer of the dress and examined the hem, giving it far more attention than it deserved. "I respond to emergency calls. I treat the patient and I get him, or her, to a hospital. Nothing much to say."

Wrong. There was so much to say, to discover.

"Did you decide on emergency medicine because of your accident? Do you enjoy your job? When did you realize emergency medicine was what you wanted to do?" Levi asked, seeing the crack in her psyche and pushing his way through.

He caught the panic in her eyes and saw her tense. Why was she feeling uncomfortable? Why did talking about her career—the one thing that should be easy to discuss—make her close up and shut down? What was he missing?

Tanna gestured to a couple of garments bags draped over the barre, a clear indication she was about to change the subject.

"Jane, the PR person, and I decided on three garment changes. I can't decide between a wool dress by Pierre Cardin which is adorned with vinyl from the late sixties, a Karl Lagerfeld and a Grès."

When he didn't respond, Tanna sent him an uncertain look and flicked her thumbnail against her chin.

She looked at the closet and flushed, and Levi lifted his eyebrows, intrigued. What was she up to now? What was she about to ask?

"Out with it, Murphy. My Chinese is getting cold." He didn't give a rat's ass about food but he was desperate to know what made this gorgeous woman blush.

"There's a dress that's amazing but…"

"But?" Levi prompted her when she stopped speaking.

"It's pretty daring. That doesn't bother me. I'm happy to show some skin…" He was okay with that too, actually. Her skin was amazing. "But I'm not sure if it suits me." Tanna cleared her throat. "If I try it on, will you tell me what you think? Will you be brutally honest?"

"Have you ever known me to be anything but honest?" he asked her.

Tanna released a small laugh. "True. Hang tight. I'm going to change as quickly as I can. Then we can eat."

Levi leaned against the wall, easily imagining Tanna moving across this floor, dressed in pink leotard and tights, her skin glistening from the exercise. Great, another fantasy to keep him awake at night. And since he already had a thousand, he really didn't need any more.

Switching mental gears, Levi wondered how long she'd danced before she gave it up. Despite spending so many hours with her while she was in the hospital, there was still a lot he didn't know about her.

He hadn't known she loved the history of fashion as much as she loved art, that she could cook pasta like an Italian mama or that her out-of-tune singing made his ears ache.

He wanted to know more. Sometimes, when he allowed his defenses to drop, he wanted to know everything.

You asked her to stay because you wanted a little revenge, some payback. Seems like the tables have turned here, Brogan.

Levi sighed, reluctantly admitting he wanted to know everything, including the noise she'd make when he slid into her and whether her skin still smelled of wild cherries, and he was desperate to discover if any other tattoos adorned her incredible body.

Tanna released a small cough and Levi pulled his eyes off the floor and onto the vision standing in front of the built-in closet in the corner of the sparsely furnished room.

Basically, her dress was a series of folds, covering the tops of her thighs and falling to the floor in a cascade of heavy cream. The top consisted of two triangles, plunging to her navel. Acres of warm, sun-kissed skin were on display and Levi, needing to hold on to something because he felt like the world was teetering, reached behind him to wrap his fingers around the barre.

Then Tanna turned around and he nearly died. Right then, his vision tunneled, and his functioning knee buckled.

There was no back to the dress and Tanna held up her heavy curls, stretching her spine, and through the gap in the side of the dress, he saw the profile of her pretty right breast.

It was official; he was down. If his leg wasn't in a cast, he'd have been on his knees, panting.

"You're killing me here, Tanna," Levi said with what was left of his breath.

Tanna dropped her hair and it tumbled down her back as she slowly, oh, so slowly, turned. "Do you like it?"

Like it? *Like* was too tame a word…but he couldn't explain his inability to speak, let alone find adequate adjectives.

"It's not vintage but there is an amazing photo of my mom in this dress and I wanted to know whether I could pull it off as well as she did," Tanna babbled. "I mean, I know I won't look as good as her, my mom was stunning, but if I can wear it, I'd like to. But I'm repeating myself… So…what do you think?"

Was she kidding him? He couldn't think, that was the goddamn problem! "Come here, Murphy."

A small frown pulled Tanna's finely arched brows together, but she collected the long skirt in her hands and lifted it halfway up her shapely calves to walk toward him.

When she was in touching distance, Levi traced the edge of her bodice with his index finger and smiled when she shivered. Still unable to speak—would he ever be able to again?—he reverently touched her collarbone and ran his fingers up her neck before pushing into those heavy curls, his hand cupping the back of her head. Her small hands rested on his chest and he watched her sexy mouth lift up to his.

Yeah, this…

He didn't understand dresses or vintage or ballet or why she was back in his life, but he didn't care. This he understood.

Levi's brain shut down when their mouths crashed and clashed. He tasted the flavor of her lip balm and swallowed her tiny moan when his tongue twisted around hers. Needing to feel her, he dropped his crutches and then his free hand was on her back, covering a good portion of her creamy, exposed skin. He danced his fingers up and down her spine, pushing under the fabric to palm her butt cheek.

God, he loved this dress.

Tanna pressed closer to him and he relished the feel of her, chest to thigh. She was a fragrant armful, a taste of heaven, the temptation of sin. Her lips were soft, her smell divine, her ability to make him as hard as titanium was a revelation.

He needed her, he wanted her…now. In this room, surrounded by mirrors where he felt overwhelmed by her, but in the best way possible.

Levi, reluctantly, pulled his mouth off hers and his hand from out of the band of the skirt. He cupped her face with both hands, his thumbs tracing the ridges of her cheekbones.

She offered him a tremulous smile. "I take it you like the dress?"

"I do." He pulled the words up, wanting to reassure

her. "You're naturally stunning, Murphy. You don't need a fancy dress to look great."

The smile grew bigger and brighter, and Levi's chest tightened.

"Trust me on this, you can pull off the dress, Tanna." He sighed and rested his forehead on hers. "It feels like I've been fighting the urge to rip the clothes off you since we stepped into this house." Another sigh. "That's a lie. I've wanted to strip you down since you walked back into my life a couple weeks ago... It has been two weeks, right?"

So much had happened and it felt like the weeks had been condensed into thirty-six hours.

Tanna's green eyes turned wicked and her mouth curved sensuously. "I'll make you a deal..."

Oh, God, his brain didn't have enough red blood cells to negotiate with this sharp-brained Murphy. He was probably about to be fleeced but he'd seen Tanna in this dress, kissed the hell out of her and could die a happy man.

"I strip for you—no ripping because this dress is, after all, couture—and then you can do whatever the hell you want with me."

Holy hell.

Levi watched as Tanna carefully removed the ivory-colored dress, revealing her wonderful skin inch by inch. The silky fabric fell down her chest and he saw, for the first time, her beautiful breasts, her taut nipples a deep, dark, rich pink, touched with spice. The fabric skimmed slim hips and as Tanna stepped out of the skirt, he noticed she was wearing a black thong. His eyes skittered over her hip and his thumb traced the long, wide scar.

"It's so ugly," Tanna whispered.

Levi shook his head. "It's your survival badge, baby."

Tanna gave him a grateful smile. Gripping the barre behind him, Levi watched through slitted eyes as Tanna draped the dress over the barre next to them before coming to stand in front of him, her hands on his hips. She stared up, and up, into his eyes and it took everything Levi had not to drag her into him, to take control of what was about to happen.

Because this had to be her decision, every step of the way.

"Do you know how often I've thought of this over the years?" she asked him, her voice, low and sensuous, sliding over him. Not as often, surely, as he had.

"I deeply regret not making love to you, Levi," Tanna said, her voice husky. "I need to know if the reality is as good as my imagination."

He did too.

Tanna played with the buttons on his shirt and he wished she'd get on with it and rip it off him. "Can I make love to you, Lee?"

It had been years since she'd called him that and it sounded good on her lips.

Maybe too good.

Levi released his grip on the barre to push a curl behind her ear. "I'll cry like a baby if you don't."

Tanna nodded but made no motion to get this show on the road. He arched an eyebrow at her. "Problem?"

"Well, yeah. You have a busted knee and a strained shoulder," Tanna said, sounding worried. "How are we going to do this? All the beds are upstairs but there are a couple of couches close by."

He didn't want to wait that long; in fact, he couldn't wait another minute. But, because he was touched by her concern, he smiled. "You don't weigh more than a feather and if you grip my hips with your legs, and I hold you with one arm, we should be able to get it done."

Levi winced. *Crap, so romantic. Try harder, Brogan.* This was Tanna, not a quick fling who was well aware of his no-commitment policy.

Instead of taking offense, Tanna giggled. "It'll have to be quick."

Levi's voice dropped to a smoky rumble. "Honey, I've wanted you for so long and so hard that being quick won't be a problem for me."

Tanna's smile flashed and then she turned her attention to his button-down shirt, slowly pulling it apart to run her hands over his chest. Levi sucked in his breath when her fingers explored his flat nipples, surprised by how sensitive they were to her touch. Inspired, he lifted his hands to her breasts, rubbing his thumbs, slowly and deliberately, across her nipples. Her eyes, still connected to his, fogged over and her breathing quickened.

Yeah, this first time wouldn't take long at all. He was already as hard as a brick and he could feel the heat wafting up from between her legs. Every inch of skin he could see was tinged with the heat of desire, her nipples were hard points begging to be touched and her eyes were full of *take me now*.

He'd done that. Levi felt awed and proud, ridiculously masculine and strangely humbled that this woman, this amazing, strong woman, was falling apart in his arms.

And they hadn't even gotten to the good part yet.

Levi hooked his finger under the thin cord around her hips and pulled her thong down her legs. When the lace lay on the floor, he looked at her perfect form and sighed. He could see her reflection in all the mirrors and each version of Tanna was better than the last. This was a memory he'd never forget.

He couldn't take the time to get properly naked. He wanted her right now; he couldn't wait a second longer.

He pushed down his pants and underwear, and Tanna immediately reached for him, but he caught her hand before she could make contact. "Don't. If you touch me, I'll blow. I'm that close."

She nodded and gripped his hip, her eyes wide with impatience. "So, what now?"

"This." Levi banded his good arm around the backs on her thighs, lifted her up and groaned when her hot mound dragged over his penis. He gritted his teeth and forced himself to concentrate. "Lock your legs behind my back and rest your calves on the barre."

Tanna did as he asked, and Levi kissed the corner of her mouth. "I'm going to slide into you and when I am deep inside you, I'm going to kiss you senseless."

Tanna's eyes flashed with hot, potent desire and a little mischief as she wound her arms around his neck, her breasts pushing into his chest. It was so hot that she was naked and he was not.

"Hell of a lot of talk happening, Brogan, not so much action."

Goaded, but also amused, Levi positioned his cock at her entrance and scraped his knuckles over her feminine folds. He saw the shock ricocheting through her eyes and she pressed down on his hand, sliding her core across the head of his penis. So...

Damn...

Good.

First times together could either be awkward, tentative or hesitant—or a combination of all three—but nothing in the way they touched, in the way they took, suggested any of that. Tanna moaned and pushed his hand away, and Levi groaned as he pushed into her warm, wet heat. God, she felt so amazing, a million times better than he'd imagined.

Reality kicked imagination's ass. And if this was revenge, he'd have more of it, thank you very much.

Needing to kiss her, to have her as close as he could get her, Levi trapped her mouth beneath his and, to hell with his shoulder, held her tight and close. He couldn't thrust, his balance was too precarious, but Tanna, obviously on the same wavelength, took control, making tiny hip movements devastating to his self-control.

He didn't need much friction, didn't need a lot of foreplay, just holding her like this, being so deeply embedded in her was enough to make his balls contract, for concentrated pleasure to build at the base of his spine.

He'd spoken the truth—this was going to be quick.

Levi gripped Tanna's butt, pushing his fingers into her soft skin. He moved from her mouth to her neck to her shoulder, sucking on her perfect skin. "Please tell me you're close, Tanna, 'cause I'm not going to be able to hang on much longer."

"Me neither."

Tanna lifted her hips, dropped back down and released a tiny scream. Her internal muscles rippled, and she clenched around him, pulsing against him. Levi lifted his head to watch her face, to watch her come, thinking he'd never seen anyone as beautiful in his life. Her skin was flushed, her lips were red from his kisses and her eyes were the fiery green of a Mogul's prize emerald.

She was utterly exquisite.

Then Tanna's channel clenched again and her small movement was it all took to release his contained pleasure, allowing it to rocket through his system, up his spine and to blow his head apart. He released a roar, angled his hips, drove deeper and smiled when Tanna orgasmed again, harder and faster than before. Yeah, he'd thought that making love to Tanna would be good, but he hadn't expected dissolve-his-knees spectacular.

Levi held her as she trembled in his arms. As his orgasm faded, his shoulder and knee were quick to remind him he'd just had sex after surgery, not even three weeks after his accident.

He didn't care.

He'd have sex, with Tanna, anytime and anywhere.

That was why they made kick-ass painkillers.

Nine

"Relax, Murphy. I'm not dead yet or even close to it."

Tanna, sitting on a chair with her elbows on her knees, immediately straightened. She hastily picked up a magazine off the floor and waved it around. "I was just reading an article on French gardens."

Levi opened his eyes to glance at the cover of the magazine. "Funny, last I heard they don't have French gardens on yachts."

Tanna looked down at the yachting magazine and silently cursed. She was so busted. Yes, she'd been watching him sleep, embarrassed by her brazen behavior in the dance studio and terrified he'd reinjured his shoulder. Or his knee. Or pulled another muscle. She didn't, after all, weigh nothing.

When they'd left the house and returned to Levi's

home on the Lockwood Estate, she could see he was in pain. Instead of his normal swinging style, he'd shuffled to the car. It was her fault. She was the medical professional. If she had been thinking straight, she would've put his rehabilitation above her sobbing libido.

"Don't you dare apologize," Levi warned her, his deep blue eyes flashing with irritation. "I was an active participant in that madness, and I could've, at any time, called it off."

Tanna sucked in her right cheek. "Why didn't you?"

"I needed to have you." Levi touched her cheekbone with the tips of his fingers, his touch light but reassuring. "Stop feeling guilty, Tanna. It doesn't suit you."

Maybe, but she and guilt were best buddies.

"But your shoulder, your knee…"

"Are fine," Levi reassured her. He must've seen the doubt in her eyes because he released a frustrated sigh. "Okay, I'm in pain, but I know I didn't do any more damage."

"Maybe we should take you to the ER to make sure?"

Levi's wicked smile turned her stomach to mush. "And how are you going to explain how I reinjured myself? Yeah, Dr. Bryce, we had wall sex."

Tanna blushed and Levi's smile widened. "Stop fussing, Murphy. I'm fine. Let's move on to another consequence of our unforgettable actions."

She wasn't sure she could deal with much more. "Okay, shoot."

Levi folded his arms across his massive chest. "We didn't use protection."

It took a few moments for his sentence to make sense. When it did, her mouth dropped open and heat rolled over her. She closed her eyes and cursed.

"I'm judging, from your reaction, that you aren't on the pill."

Tanna shook her head. "Nope."

Levi nodded, looking remarkably sanguine. "So, you could, maybe, become pregnant?"

Tanna ran through her cycle and lifted her hand to rock it back and forth. "I think I'll be okay. We're just out of the window."

"So, there is a chance?"

"A small one," Tanna conceded. "But, if your sperm is already charming my egg, I'm up the river without a paddle." Panic flashed in her eyes, chased by fear.

"Okay, the look on your face is starting to scare me," Levi said.

"I can't be pregnant, Levi. I don't want a baby! If I'm pregnant, I'll be tied to you, tied to Boston."

Wow.

He didn't think he could still be hurt by Tanna, but yep, apparently he was wrong about that.

Levi tipped his head to the side. "Is being pregnant really the worst thing that can happen, Tanna? Being a mother, living in Boston…"

Being around me? Seeing where this is going?

What the hell was wrong with him? Why was he walking down this road again? Tanna had made her feelings clear a decade ago and nothing had changed.

He hadn't understood her then, and ten years on, he was still fumbling around in the dark.

"Maybe I should explain," Tanna quietly stated and it was only then that Levi realized he'd spoken out loud. "I need you to understand…it wasn't you but me."

This crap again? "Isn't that the standard line?"

Tanna spread her hands. "Maybe. But, in my case, it's pure truth. When I left Boston, I flew to London and I moved in with Padma, my godmother. I was a bit of a wreck." Tanna paused. "I know you won't believe me, but leaving was hard for me, Levi."

Yeah, he didn't believe it. Or maybe he didn't want to believe it. Who knew?

Tanna started to speak, stopped and pushed her hand into her long hair. She stared at the TV set on the wall opposite and he waited for her to continue.

They might as well get this done and out of the way.

"So, I was in London, missing you, missing my brothers, missing my home. After a week of crying, Padma, who is as tough as she is sweet, told me I couldn't just lie about, I had to do something. So, I went traveling. When I returned to London two years later, Padma sat me down again and demanded to know what I wanted to do with the rest of my life, where I was going, what I was going to do when I got there," Tanna said. "You never met Padma but I know you'd love her. And she'd flirt with you."

Her eyes met his and her smile pushed his world off its axis, shifted magnetic north. God, that was another thing he'd forgotten…the way her eyes lightened, her face brightened, how her smile dimmed the power of the sun.

"I knew I couldn't return to Boston or join Murphy's."

"Couldn't? Why not?"

Tanna took a long time to answer. "It felt frivolous. It *still* feels frivolous. Back then, I couldn't see myself going back to Murphy's when everything else had changed. I also couldn't stop thinking that, if you hadn't called 911 when you did, if the EMTs weren't as quick as they were, I might have, like Addy, died that night. It really worried me that I didn't know what to do in an emergency if someone needed my help. So I decided to do a first-aid course. I loved it, so I did another. Within a few years, I was pretty highly qualified."

Levi listened, fascinated by her story. He'd had first-hand experience of her determination, so he could easily imagine Tanna applying her mind to her studies. "I finally felt like I was contributing, like I was doing something important, and then I joined HART."

"Heart?"

Tanna enunciated the individual letters. "*H-A-R-T* is the Hazardous Area Response Team. They recruit and train selected emergency personnel who respond to major incidents."

Levi frowned. "What sort of major incidents?"

"Train crashes, large-scale motorway accidents, building collapses or significant fires. Terrorism incidents, bomb blasts, that type of thing. HART doesn't respond to your normal, run-of-the-mill accident,"

Tanna explained. "Basically, we go into all the hot zones."

His worst nightmare. Levi couldn't think of anything worse than one of his loved ones constantly walking into danger and being unable to protect them. Thank God, and all his minions, he and Tanna weren't together anymore.

He'd wouldn't be able to function knowing she was walking into a situation out of his control.

"I was the youngest, and least experienced, recruit in fifteen years. They looked at my injuries and told me there was no way I'd pass the fitness exam, but I did. They told me they doubted I'd pass the psychological exam, given the trauma I experienced, but I did. The survival drills were the toughest—white-water rafting, abseiling, crawling through a tunnel in the dark with my kit—but I got through it."

He could see she was waiting for him to say something, to praise her efforts, and he should; her achievements were incredibly impressive, especially given how broken she'd been just a few years before. But he couldn't form the words because the urge to pick her up and shake her, to demand to know why she was putting herself at risk—after barely surviving a bad accident—was like a hot, violent river of lava.

How dare she play with her safety? How dare she place herself in danger again?

Levi opened his mouth to blast her but knowing he didn't have the right—his ring wasn't on her finger—he dropped his head back to stare at the ceiling. His sisters were always on him about being too protective and he knew that if he ripped into Tanna, she'd shut down and this conversation would end.

Knowing it was smarter to keep his mouth shut, he gritted his teeth. It was hard but he managed it. Just.

He folded his arms and dug his fingers into his biceps. "Okay, so you joined this specialized team…"

"I finally felt like I was where I was supposed to be. I started in emergency medicine because I wanted to give something back and I joined HART because I felt like I had a bigger part to play, because the work is relevant. I guess I needed to prove to myself I was more than a PR person, that I was more than a broken body lying in that hospital bed," Tanna added.

"Of course you were more," Levi protested, unable to believe she'd felt that way.

"No, you don't understand!" Tanna pushed both hands into her hair and gripped the long strands in her fingers. "Before the accident, Levi, I lived this charmed life. Sure, I lost my folks young, but I had three gorgeous, strong, dedicated brothers who made me their entire world. School was easy for me. I was pretty, rich, smart and popular. I got into an Ivy League college without trying very hard."

"You also had an accident that nearly took your life."

"But it didn't," Tanna said, her eyes bubbling with raw emotion. "I should've died but I didn't. I should not have been able to walk, but I did. I even, somehow, managed to find a handsome, gorgeous man, who stood by me and then proposed marriage. Who does that happen to?"

"You, apparently," Levi pointed out.

"I realized I've never really been challenged, that everything came to me so easily."

She'd nearly died and had endured months of pain after many surgeries. Why did she keep forgetting that part?

"Before the accident I'd never stood on my own two feet, never had to make a hard decision, never faced anything difficult at all."

Wasn't the trick to life to enjoy the good times and avoid the hard? Or had he missed something?

Tanna put her hands into the back pockets of her jeans and rocked on her heels, looking young and vulnerable. "Becoming an EMT was tough. There were so many times I wanted to give up. But it's good work, Levi, important work."

She stared at her feet, her face pale. "And I think Addy would like the fact that I'm doing something worthwhile, contributing."

Levi leaned forward, seeing something in her eyes suggesting deep sadness and an ocean's worth of guilt. "What do you mean by that, Tan?"

"She'd appreciate the fact that I'm no longer some little rich girl who needs her burly brothers or sexy fiancé to take care of her. Addy was so independent, she'd applaud me for making my own way. That I'm doing something important, something to make the world a little better. After all, she's not here to do it herself."

Levi held up his hand, shocked by the suspicion forming in his brain. "Tan, it's not your fault she died."

Tanna glared at him. "Oh, please, of course it is.

She was driving my fast, powerful car because I was drunk. Because I had too much of a party, too much fun. She died because of me, Levi."

It had been an accident, an unfortunate series of events, and if Tanna had gotten behind the wheel drunk, she could've killed herself and a dozen other people. His heart ached for her; she'd thought she was doing the right thing by not driving under the influence, but the evening still ended in someone dying.

How utterly, profoundly sad was that?

"Honey, you've got to give yourself a break."

"Life didn't give Addy a break so I'm not entitled to one either."

Tanna took a step back and Levi knew she was regretting her words, that she'd said too much. Before he could push her for more, to talk this through with her, to make her see how tough she was being on herself, she abruptly spun around and left the room. Thirty seconds later he heard her footsteps running up the stairs.

He started to go after her but quickly remembered he couldn't follow her up the stairs.

He was so over being injured. If he could, he'd rip his cast off with his bare hands.

"Can I get you something to drink?"

Thankfully, Tanna wasn't one to sulk and she was back downstairs in thirty minutes, her eyes red but her expression composed.

Levi rubbed his hands over his face, wishing she had a bit more color to hers. He'd do anything to strip the exhaustion from her expression and the haunted look from her eyes. She wasn't as together as he'd thought she was, and neither was he.

His plan for revenge, a little payback and keeping his distance had gone to hell.

And that might be because they were digging too deep, picking at sores long healed. The past was the past and couldn't be changed or fixed, and he wasn't the type to look back. Neither was he the type to look forward, not when it came to relationships.

He had to remember he and Tanna had a past but they had no future. They only had the present and he didn't want to spend their time together arguing about things that couldn't be changed.

He—they—needed control and they needed it now. It was time for a reset.

"Come here, Tan."

Tanna crossed the room and when she was close enough, he reached for her arm, gently wrapping his fingers around her delicate wrist and tugging her toward him. Tanna looked down at him and he smiled at her defiant, proud expression. "Honey, I don't want to fight with you."

She didn't look convinced.

Levi's thumb traced the soft skin of her inner wrist. "You're here for another few weeks and I don't think rehashing the past is a productive use of our time."

Amusement tinged with relief touched her eyes and her lips, and Levi knew he was gaining ground.

"And I suppose you have a couple of ideas of how productive we can be?"

He patted his thigh. "If you sit down, I could show you what I had in mind."

Tanna flipped her legs over his hips to straddle him, her hair falling down the side of her face and tickling his chin.

"Looks like you have some ideas of your own," Levi said, his hand tucking her hair behind her ear.

Tanna nibbled the side of his jaw, her teeth scraping his three-day beard. "Oh, I have a few."

"I'm happy to consider them." Levi ran his hand down her back, cupped her butt and squeezed. This was all that was important, the here and the now of being able to touch her. He wanted slow, he wanted sexy, he wanted to wring every ounce of pleasure from her.

But, like before, they didn't have any condoms. They'd taken a hell of a risk earlier and he wasn't about to spin the barrel of that loaded revolver again.

He also couldn't, wouldn't, let there be any misunderstandings between them. Gripping her biceps, he gently pushed her up and back, to sit her on his thighs.

Confusion flashed in Tanna's eyes. "Problem?"

"We need condoms."

Tanna slapped her hand against her forehead, obviously embarrassed she'd forgotten about protection again.

"What the hell is wrong with me? Okay, condoms." She wrinkled her nose. "I don't have any. Do you?"

Yeah, he had a box upstairs. Levi told her where to find them but, as she started to climb off him, he gripped her hips to keep her in place.

Tanna sighed her frustration and lifted her eyebrows to give him a *what now?* look.

When she'd strolled back into his life with her lithe body and gorgeous face, he'd wanted revenge, payback, for her to beg for his forgiveness. Now all he could think about was protecting himself, making sure he didn't start to fall for her again.

Because he could only be that stupid once.

Levi stroked her arm from shoulder to wrist, making sure to keep eye contact. "We always found it easy to talk to each other, Tan, but it's not a good idea."

She immediately caught his drift. Nobody could ever accuse Tanna of being slow. "Because it feels a bit too real, huh? Too much like what we had?"

Levi nodded. "I can't go back there, Tanna."

Tanna's shoulders slumped. "Me neither."

"I want you, but I don't want you thinking we can go anywhere with this," Levi added.

"I know. I'm the one who is leaving, remember? As soon as I—" She stopped talking abruptly and stared past him.

As soon as she what? Levi started to ask and cursed himself when he remembered what he'd said not a minute before. He had to stop asking her questions that led to deeper conversations.

Tanna waved her comment away. "Forget it. It doesn't matter."

It did. Everything she thought or felt was important. He didn't want it to be, but it was.

"I still want to sleep with you," Levi said. Sex was all they could have.

He expected her to retreat, to slide off his lap, but Tanna just looked at him with clear eyes. "I still want that too."

Levi released the breath he'd been holding when Tanna finally climbed off his lap. Okay, good, still on the same page.

At the door, Tanna turned and her smile was a brain-stopping combination of sweet and seductive. "You said the condoms are on the top shelf of your bathroom cabinet?"

Thank you, baby Jesus. Sex he could do, but this emotional BS? Not so much.

Or at all.

Ten

Carrick stood at the entrance to the viewing room and watched as Tanna directed the maintenance staff on how to hang the huge photographs of Raeni in dresses very similar to the ones on sale. He had to admit that Levi's idea to link the sale with his stepmom and have Tanna wear Raeni's dresses was fantastic. Murphy's was now expecting a bigger crowd than before.

Excellent news.

Somehow, without managing to upset his head of PR, Jane, or any other staff, Tanna had taken over all the arrangements for the presale cocktail party. Her antipathy toward Murphy International seemed to have vanished and Carrick often found her about the place, in this viewing room or in Jane's office. Or on the phone to a potential buyer or chatting to a vendor.

When he asked her why she was spending her vacation time in Murphy's, working, she blithely told him she liked being there and she needed to find something to fill her hours while Levi was at work. He might've believed her if she'd been able to meet his eyes while speaking.

Tanna was lying about being back in Boston on vacation and he would, eventually, find out why. And Levi spending more and more hours at work worried Carrick. He was pretty sure Levi shouldn't be so mobile yet.

He was also sure Levi and Tanna were getting naked. If Levi was up for sex, he could handle going to work.

Carrick was glad someone was getting lucky because he as sure as hell wasn't.

Sadie Slade's stunning face flashed into his mind and Carrick closed his eyes, thinking of a math equation to stop him from embarrassing himself.

Damn, now he was getting turned on at work? He'd had a couple of X-rated dreams about the art detective and he'd woken up sweaty and disorientated and needing, literally, to take himself in hand.

That hadn't happened to him since he was in his teens and it annoyed him that Sadie had that much power over him. Until he got his craving for her under control, he was avoiding her.

Because, apparently, he had all the maturity and sophistication of a fifteen-year-old.

Carrick pushed his hand through his hair and, realizing standing around wasn't productive, decided to return to his office where he could, he was sure, still smell Sadie's perfume in the air.

Carrick felt a hand on his shoulder and whipped around to see Levi behind him, still on crutches. He smiled as they exchanged fist bumps.

"Tanna asked if I would send a driver to fetch you," Carrick told him, looking at his watch. "But in an hour or so."

"My orthopedic surgeon had a cancellation so he could see me earlier. I caught a taxi here." Levi nodded to Tanna, who was on a stepladder, holding a huge photograph of her mom. "Is she being as bossy as hell?"

Carrick grinned at the affection in Levi's voice. "She is."

Levi looked around the room, his gaze bouncing off the massive arrangements of flowers, and frowned. "Where are the dresses, the items that are going to be on sale?"

"Ah, well, my bossy sister decided that, instead of using mannequins to display the dresses, she would hire live models to parade the clothes and the jewelry. The clothing is presently being allocated to models and there are about a dozen in the conference room, half naked."

Levi grinned and grabbed his crutches. "Remind me where the conference room is?"

Carrick smiled. "Ha ha. Anyway, Tanna has blown the budget to hell and back."

"I know you and you're not even a little annoyed. Why not?" Levi asked.

"I suppose that's because I'm so damn happy to see

her in Murphy's, having fun." Carrick sighed. "And she's also persuaded at least ten of the world's biggest collectors to personally attend the cocktail party and the auction. Because they are coming, we've had a lot more interest in the sale. Their presence will drive the prices up, so how can I complain about her being over budget?"

"Your sister has a way of overturning apple carts," Levi commented.

"Is that what she's doing to you?" Carrick asked.

Levi stared at Tanna, who was still up on the ladder, before turning to face Carrick. He shook his head. "Get that idea out of your head, Murph. It's not going to happen. We're just friends."

Pfft. Sure they were. Just like Carrick didn't want Sadie Slade with his next breath.

And, talking about the good doctor of art history, he turned around to see her approaching him, dressed in another of her bohemian business outfits. Today she wore a tiny, Aztec-inspired miniskirt and a flame-colored jacket skimming slim hips over a bright cobalt blue silk shirt. Her heels showed off her gorgeous legs.

Yep, tonight would be another long, long, night.

Sadie smiled at him and he was certain his heart stopped, just for a minute. She gestured to the viewing room and, after greeting Levi, asked whether she could look inside.

Carrick stood aside to let her pass and she stared at the large room, disappointment on her face. "I really wanted to see the dresses and the jewelry."

"Come to the cocktail party tomorrow night," Carrick impulsively suggested.

Excitement jumped into Sadie's eyes and Carrick felt heat invade his veins. Yep, it was official; he'd do just about anything to see her smile. After his marriage fell apart, he'd vowed to keep his love life uncomplicated and surface based. Sadie was testing that vow.

"Are you sure?" she asked.

Carrick nodded. "I'll email you an invitation."

"That's great, thanks. I presume it's formal?"

"Black tie," Carrick confirmed, unable to pull his eyes off her sexy, wide mouth. He was vaguely aware of Tanna approaching him and he finally yanked his gaze away, helped by Levi's elbow in his ribs.

"God, you are so pathetic," Levi muttered out of the side of his mouth.

"Pot. Kettle. Black," Carrick retorted as he watched his sister and the woman he wanted to sleep with exchange greetings and knew he was in for a world of hurt.

So, judging by the look on Levi's face, was his best friend.

On Friday morning, Tanna drained her coffee and turned to Levi, who'd just finished his daily call to his marina manager. Or one of his managers as there were many calls, every morning.

"I have an appointment in the city," Tanna informed him. "Then I have a hair appointment this afternoon so I'm not going to be around a lot today. And tonight is the Murphy cocktail party."

A small frown pulled Levi's eyebrows together. "This is the third appointment you've had this week. Are you sick or something?"

Please don't pry, Tanna silently begged him. *I don't want to lie to you but I'm not ready to talk about this, not yet. Probably not ever.*

"I'm fine."

Levi sent her his patented you're-BS-ing-me look. "What's going on, Tanna?"

Tanna picked up her phone and swiped the screen, hoping he'd take the hint that she didn't want to discuss this further.

Levi's hand caught her wrist and she was forced to look at him. Tense and annoyed, she returned his hard look. "Why are you pushing this, Levi? It's not relevant to…us."

Levi released her and annoyance flashed across his face. "Tanna, you have bad dreams. I hear them. You wake up often and you talk in your sleep. Something is going on with you and I want to know what it is."

After telling her that there was no point in rehashing the past, why was he pushing her? And if she had to answer, what would she say?

I'm suffering from PTSD and my career is on the line. I've been placed on medical leave and I might lose my job—the job I need so I can live with myself—if I don't get myself under control. This isn't something you or anyone else can fix. And I will fix it. I'm not the girl you used to know who needs her big, tough fiancé to solve her problems.

So, no, that was far too personal and she couldn't share any of that.

"Does it have something to do with your job? Why are you taking a six-week break? And don't tell me it's a vacation. I'm not buying that."

He didn't understand; spending time with him and at Murphy's *was* a vacation...

She'd loved every minute she'd spent talking art and design and jewelry. When she went back to London, she'd be faced with injury and death, making quick, hard decisions in an instant. Work wasn't fun, but it was good, *necessary*.

"What part of 'I'm fine' don't you understand, Brogan?" Tanna demanded, annoyed. She made a show of glancing at her watch. "I'm going to shower and get changed—"

"Why won't you talk about your job? About why you are really here in Boston?"

More questions, Brogan?

Aargh, she didn't have time for this. And no, she didn't want to explain that, ten years after her accident, all the trauma she'd experienced then was rushing back to torment her again. She'd had counseling sessions; she'd thought she'd dealt with this emotional mess.

But the flashbacks and panic attacks were from the PTSD. Her therapist had told her that unresolved issues were lingering deep inside her. Those were the issues she'd come to Boston to face.

Reining in her impatience, she made herself smile. "I don't talk about my job because most people don't want to hear about broken bones and heart attacks."

And because every time she thought about returning to her position at HART, her stomach clenched and her throat tightened. It was ridiculous; she was stronger than this. Not returning to London wasn't an option. She would not let this beat her.

The muscle in Levi's jaw ticked and Tanna knew he was trying to understand. She waited for him to resume speaking and when he did, he surprised her with his next question. "Do you enjoy being a paramedic?"

Tanna looked at him, shocked. Of course, she did. She hadn't studied long and hard for the fun of it. "Yes, of course."

Levi didn't look convinced. "Tell me something you love about your job, something that gives you a kick every time you do it." He held up a hand. "And don't say *when I save a life*. That's too easy."

Saving a life had been the first thing that popped into her head. "I don't understand what you're getting at."

Levi tapped his index finger against the wooden tabletop. "Okay, let me give you an example. It's a little silly but when a yacht leaves the marina, I immediately check the visitor's book to see what they said about their stay. I get some damn good reviews and it gives me a kick. That's one of my many little joys. Tell me one of yours."

Tanna looked at him, askance. Crap, she couldn't remember any of the little joys. Her job was filled with lots of downtime punctuated by sessions of intense concentration and craziness. She'd always been consumed by the feeling she was doing something worthwhile, something important, so she never stopped to notice the joys. She only noticed the successes, and that was decidedly different...

"Can't answer, huh? Okay, then answer me this..."

Tanna forced herself to meet his eyes and they drilled through her, pinning her to the floor. His expression, and his tone, reflected the seriousness of his question.

"Do you actually like what you do, Murphy? Did you ever?"

She couldn't answer him; the question was too big and too direct and too honest. She didn't want to continue this conversation because if Levi pushed her to dig, to question her own motivations, she might not like her answers.

Besides, it didn't matter whether she enjoyed her job or not, it was what she had to do in order to live with herself, to live with the guilt of Addy's death.

It was way past time to shut this down... They weren't supposed to be talking, anyway.

Gathering her courage, she walked around the table and dragged her mouth across his lips, pulling back to see the desire flash in his eyes. She kissed him again, allowing her tongue to slide into his mouth. Levi immediately reached for her and dragged her onto his lap, her legs straddling his hips and his erection settling between her thighs.

Tanna deepened the kiss, grateful men were so easily distracted.

Levi took control of their kiss and soon Tanna had forgotten his question, sinking into his hard body, entranced by his strength and captivated by his kisses. Levi had the ability to pull her into another dimension, a world where nothing existed but their passion and need to make each other feel as good as possible.

They didn't need to talk, they just needed to touch.

Then Levi put his hands on her shoulders and gently pushed her away. Tanna looked at him through passion-fogged eyes and wondered why he'd stopped.

Levi ran his thumb over her bottom lip. "I know you were trying to distract me but I'm not a kid anymore. You didn't answer my question, Murphy."

And she wouldn't. Frustrated and a little annoyed at being called out, she climbed off Levi's strong thighs and sent him a cool smile. "I'm going to shower and then I'm going into the city. I'll see you when I see you."

"You are so damn frustrating," Levi told her as she walked away.

Since she had to live with herself, his statement wasn't even news.

"Mrs. Talbot." Tanna held out her hand to the matriarch of Boston society, her blood so blue it was almost purple, and dropped a kiss on each of her leathery cheeks. "I haven't seen you since I was a child."

Mrs. Frieda Talbot, as old as God, looked at Tanna with eyes that had lived a million lives. "I remember you wearing pigtails, sitting in the corner of Carrick's office while we conducted business."

Frieda was one of Murphy's oldest and wealthiest clients, owning both extensive art and jewelry collections. Addicted to spending money, she received an invitation to every function and auction Murphy's held.

"It's so lovely to see you. Do you have an eye on anything special?" Tanna asked her.

"I rather fancy the flower purse, circa 1930. I think the estimate is a bit high at five hundred dollars."

Tanna smiled, remembering Frieda had once purchased a Willem de Kooning for more than three million dollars. Frieda liked what she liked and was always looking for a bargain.

"I hope you get it," Tanna told her sincerely. "And at a satisfactory price."

Frieda seemed pleased by her statement and, her attention caught by an old friend, abruptly left Tanna. Tanna grinned and turned at the light tap on her shoulder.

Pulling a polite smile onto her face—everybody present wanted to talk to her about her mom's dresses or her mom or fashion in general—Tanna turned and her smile widened in genuine pleasure.

"Sadie, it's so nice to see you. I love your dress."

In fact, with its white bodice and short skirt trimmed with flowers, it looked a lot like the Christian Dior in the sale.

"It's a cheap knockoff," Sadie admitted. "I found it in a little boutique in Paris. The owner slash designer takes her inspiration from the sixties."

"You look wonderful."

"You do too," Sadie replied. "I've loved every dress you've worn tonight but this one is simply sensational."

Tanna couldn't help it; she looked across the room

to where Levi stood by the bar, leaning on his crutches and talking to Finn. When she looked down at the ivory crepe, she remembered stepping out of it in the dance studio at the Beacon Hill house, being naked while Levi was still fully dressed.

This dress made her hot…

Oh, Lord, who was she kidding? Levi made her hot. All the freakin' time.

Tanna accepted a martini from a passing waiter and tossed a large portion of the drink down her throat, thinking she'd never had so much sex in her life…

And every single time, Levi made it magical. Even with his limited movement. God help her if she ever got to make love to him when he was fully mobile. She might not survive.

But she'd be long gone before that happened. She had to keep her eye on her goal, on what she needed to do. Her plan was to get healthy and return to her job.

Playing house with Levi wasn't her real life. That had been a teenager's dream and it had been a long time since she'd been a teenager, or a dreamer. Tanna looked at Sadie's flower ring, thinking that leaving Levi, again, was going to be hard, possibly even harder than before. Because, while she knew she had to go back to her job and her life in London, she'd enjoyed playing house with her ex-fiancé. It had given her a taste of how her life could've been had she taken the easy route and married Levi.

And, dammit, a huge part of her felt a little sick about all she'd missed out on with him. The years of sharing his home and his bed, loving and laughing and fighting and making up.

But, had she married Levi, her life, their lives, would've been tainted by her guilt, by her *what-ifs* and her *should haves*. How would she have been able to live such a wonderful life when Addy had been stripped of hers?

And if Tanna got a little carried away, thinking she could easily fall in love with Levi again—had she even stopped loving him?—she still wasn't entitled to live a fairy-tale life.

No, she had to pay for the choices she'd made. And she was paying, dammit.

She was just taking a little time out, having a few weeks of fun and a lot of great sex. In a few weeks, she'd return to her real, gritty, emotionally draining job and her quiet life in London. But for now, yeah, she was going to enjoy the hell out of Levi Brogan.

"Wow, that was a hell of a side trip," Sadie said, smiling. "I want some of whatever put that faraway look in your eyes."

Tanna just smiled, wishing she and Sadie were good enough friends that she could share the truth, that she was overdosing on great sex. Her eyes darted to Levi and he almost immediately turned his head, and their eyes clashed and connected. Even though they were at opposite ends of the room, she could feel the intensity of his gaze, and knew exactly what he was thinking…

Your dress is coming off, sooner rather than later.

Levi jerked his head in a subtle come-here movement and Tanna, liking the adventurous light in his eyes, excused herself from Sadie.

Instead of waiting for her, Levi headed to the door and quickly—man, he could move on those crutches— disappeared through the door leading from the cocktail lounge into the hallway.

Despite trying to dodge people wanting to talk to her, Tanna greeted Murphy's clients, exchanged kisses and hugs, and kept the conversations super short. But it was still more than ten minutes before she slipped out the door into the hallway of the hotel and Levi was nowhere to be seen. Needing a minute to catch her breath, she walked toward the elevators, looking for the ladies' room. Seeing the discreet sign, she headed to the end of the hall, holding her long skirt off the carpet.

She was a few yards from the restroom when a door to her right opened and a strong arm wrapped around her waist and pulled her up against a hard chest.

Levi's mouth covered hers as he stepped back, and she dimly heard the door slam behind him.

Pulling her mouth off his, she noticed they were in a small lounge, perfect for a two-person meeting. Levi leaned against the door and reached behind him to flip the lock.

Oh, God, she'd heard about people who sneaked away from functions for a little naughtiness, but like joining the mile-high club, she'd never expected it to happen to her. Judging by the very hard erection tenting Levi's pants, however, that was exactly what was going to happen.

She was so on board.

"Have I told you how sexy you look tonight? How much I love this dress?" Levi demanded, his lips on her bare shoulder.

No, but since he'd made love to her before leaving the house, carefully removing the dress, she'd gotten the message.

"I freaking *love* this dress."

Tanna laughed. "I got the hint." She looped her arms around his neck and crossed her wrists behind his head. "I was hoping you'd do this."

"Make out with you in an empty room in the middle of a cocktail party?" Levi asked, his tongue tracing the cord in her neck.

Tanna shivered and pushed her fingers into his soft hair. "Yeah. It's…hot," Tanna admitted, blushing. Levi had the ability to make her rocket from zero to about-to-come in ten seconds flat. "Whenever we are together, I feel like I'm permanently connected to an electrical socket."

Levi lifted his head and his thumb rubbed her lower lip. "Is that a good or bad thing?"

"You know it's a good thing, Lee," Tanna whispered. In fact, everything about him was, well, pretty damn wonderful. No matter what limits he'd tried to place on their conversations, in between making love they talked, and unlike before, they connected on the same intellectual wavelength. There was a balance now…

"Do you want me to touch you?" Levi asked her, his voice rough with need.

He always asked for permission and never assumed

he had the right to make love to her. Tanna knew it was his way of keeping an emotional distance between them, a certain barrier.

Levi was still waiting for an answer and Tanna nodded. "Please touch me, Lee. Make love to me, here. Now. Immediately."

"I want to, you know I do, but you're in the public eye tonight and if I do, everyone—including your brothers—will know what we did." Levi held her nape, his thumb stroking her jaw. "I'm not going to embarrass you like that, babe."

"Aargh." Tanna dropped her forehead to rest it on Levi's collarbone. "So, why did you haul me in here, then?"

"Because I couldn't stand being across the room and not being able to hold you, kiss you. Acting like we are just platonic friends is killing me," Levi responded. "And if your brothers find out we've hooked up, they will kill me. Though I think Carrick suspects something is going on."

"It has nothing to do with them," Tanna told him, instantly annoyed. Her life, her body, her choice...

"Yeah, trust me, that's not the way brothers work, babe." Levi tipped her face up and his lips touched hers in a kiss as sweet as it was sexy. "Need you, Tan. Again. It's too much, isn't it?"

Tanna agreed. It really was. But she'd take this type of too much.

Holding Levi's face in her hands, her mouth softened under his, and their kiss was languid, lovely, soft and liquid. Passion was there, underneath the sweet, but was banked, and they both knew if they allowed it to run rampant, they'd lose control. So Tanna matched his pace, their tongues tangling softly, their hands moving lightly across each other's bodies. Tanna sighed as his hand slid inside the triangle covering her right breast, his fingers flickering over her nipple, barely touching her but stunningly sexy.

She groaned into his mouth, wanting to take it deeper, harder, but Levi shook his head. "Got to go slow, babe. Got to keep this light."

Right, cocktail party, people outside, appearances to keep up.

Levi's hand skimmed over her hip, down her thigh and under the high slit of her dress, his hand disappearing under the flowing folds. She sucked in her breath when his fingers found the edge of her panties and she immediately undid his tuxedo jacket, looking for the snap on his pants.

Levi's strong hand covered hers. "Nope. This isn't about me."

What? Her hand stilled, wanting to stroke the large bulge beneath her hand. "But…"

"Slow, sexy and only one of us is going to come. And guess what?" Levi whispered against her lips.

"What?"

"It isn't going to be me."

His words were barely out of his mouth when his fingers pulled down her flesh-colored panties and sank into her folds. Like before, his touch was gentle, soft, and Tanna couldn't believe how turned on she was.

He'd just need to flick her, a couple of strokes and she'd be flying.

How? How did he do this?

"Do you want to get off, Tan? Right here, right now? As gently as hell and twice as sexy?"

He didn't need to do anything, he just needed to rumble words against her skin, and she was already there. "Please, Lee."

Levi took her mouth again and his tongue echoed the soft, gentle movements of his fingers as they slid inside her. Only Levi could touch her like this, could make her churn and yearn…

Tanna felt herself building, climbing, pleasure—this time a soft, gentle wave as opposed to a passion-driven tsunami—washing over her.

Tanna pushed down on his fingers and he curled them into her, hitting a special spot she hadn't known existed until Levi taught her it was there. He also ran his thumb over that little bundle of nerves. It was all too much and Tanna stilled, pulled her mouth from Levi's, her entire body focused on what he was doing between her legs.

The wave rose, heated her from the inside out, and she tumbled, falling, spinning, rolling…

All the colors of a spectacular coral reef exploded in her brain and she slapped her hand against Levi's chest, hoping he'd realize she couldn't stand, that she could hardly breathe.

Nothing else, besides what he was doing to her, mattered. Levi banded his other arm around her, held her steady as he pushed her to reach for more, to own her pleasure, to fall into it. She came again, screamed softly and disintegrated in his arms.

Tanna had no idea how long it took her to fall back into reality, a place she didn't want to return to, but she had to return when Levi pulled his hand away. Then his strong arms cuddled her close and she could feel his nose in her hair, his lips against her temple.

"God, Tanna. You're so damn beautiful."

Tanna closed her eyes and let his words wash over her.

"Why do I have to be so damn addicted you?"

Dammit, how the hell was she going to walk away from him, from this again? She'd done it once, but back then she hadn't known the power of his touch, how utterly satisfied she felt standing in his arms. Oh, not just because he gave her amazing orgasms, but because he saw her.

He saw her as she was now, today. Strong. Independent. Confident.

Leaving was something she had to do.

Wasn't it?

"Tanna? Where are you?"

Tanna jerked her head back at the loud shout from the hallway. She saw the *WTF?* look in Levi's eyes, knowing she hadn't imagined the panic in Carrick's voice.

"Tanna, I need you, dammit!" Carrick's voice was a loud roar outside the door.

Levi spun around, opened the door behind him to Carrick, whose face was ashen beneath his tan.

Tanna placed a hand on her brother's arm, her nails digging in to grab his attention. "Carrick! What's the problem?"

"It's Sadie. I think she's choking. You need to come."

Tanna didn't hesitate; she just kicked off her shoes, lifted her skirts and started to run.

Eleven

The doors to the ambulance had barely closed when the driver accelerated, desperate to take Sadie, who was still breathing via a pen tube jammed into her throat, to the nearest emergency room. Tanna felt Finn's arm around her waist and Ronan's big body shielding her from the freezing wind. Soft fabric enveloped her and Tanna looked down to see Ronan's jacket on her bare shoulders.

Ronan placed his hand on her back. "Honey, you need to get inside. Your feet must be freezing."

Tanna looked down, suddenly realizing she couldn't feel her toes. Coming back to where she was—standing on the cold stone steps leading up to the hotel's front door—she looked around and blinked.

"Where's Levi?" she asked, as Ronan and Finn escorted her back into the lobby of the iconic Forrester-Grantham hotel. Tanna saw the strange looks she was getting and shrugged. Let people talk—what did she care? She wouldn't be staying in Boston so what people said didn't worry her.

"We're not sure, honey," Finn gently told her.

She looked up into Finn's face and blinked back her tears, not wanting to hurt him by telling him that, while she appreciated his support, she wanted Levi.

Right. Damn. Now.

"I'll go up to the function room and see whether he's still there," Ronan offered.

Tanna watched Ronan walk away and stared down at the grubby, wet hem of her dress and her blue feet. She felt like she was operating outside of herself, like she was watching herself go through the motions.

"Are you okay, Tan?" Finn asked, obviously concerned.

She really wasn't.

She was going to toss her cookies—and her champagne and those delicious canapés—right now.

Breathing through her nose, Tanna counted to ten, then to twenty, pushing the nausea away. Images of the past twenty minutes floated through her brain, Sadie lying on her back, her eyes wide and terrified, gagging from the obstruction in her throat. Her hand fluttered around her neck, silently begging Tanna to help her.

Tanna's training kicked in and she'd started barking orders like a drill sergeant. By the time she was done, she'd performed an emergency tracheotomy and Sadie was breathing again, her blue eyes wide and scared.

Tanna hadn't panicked or seen dots in front of her eyes or battled to breathe. No, she'd remained calm and cool and in control, doing what she needed to do, what she'd committed her life to doing. She'd saved Sadie's life, just like she'd saved other lives in other situations.

Addy was still dead, but Tanna was paying it forward as best she could. This was what she was supposed to do. Working at Murphy's was lovely, fun and light and fluffy, but it wasn't important, imperative. Saving lives was.

And she'd done it. Without a single PTSD symptom.

Tanna felt Levi's heat and then his big arms came around her, cuddling her close. Tanna turned, buried her face in his chest and wrapped her arms around his waist, wishing she could slide inside him.

"Well done, Tan. You saved her life."

"Can't stop shaking," Tanna told him, feeling tears slip down her face.

"I've got you." Levi stroked her back, up into her hair, his hands and body warming her as Ronan's designer jacket couldn't do. Handing her shoes to Finn, his strong arm around her waist, he led her to a sofa in a secluded corner of the lobby and sat down, pulling her onto his lap. Tanna buried her face in his neck and just cried harder, her sobs coming out as a series of hiccups.

She normally only fell apart when she was alone, when she was guaranteed her privacy. But this was different, she wasn't seeing Addy, she couldn't smell blood, she wasn't back in her long-ago car, her legs pinned by metal.

She wasn't crying because of the PTSD, she was crying because, this time, for the first time, she recognized herself again, as the EMT she'd been for so many years. She'd done what she needed to do, quickly, efficiently.

She'd saved Sadie's life. And maybe, just maybe, her PTSD symptoms had left as quickly as they'd arrived.

Tanna wasn't sure how long she cried. It could've been for two minutes or twenty, but eventually Levi patted her back and commanded her to stop. The combination of his sharp tone and the light grip of his fingers on her shoulder snapped her head up and she stared at him through waterlogged eyes.

"I don't understand—this is what you do. This is what you trained for," Levi said. "You've been in worse situations than this, Tanna, surely?"

Tanna nodded. "Yeah, obviously."

"Then I don't understand your reaction, the tears and the falling apart," Levi said, thoroughly confused.

Tanna wiped her tears away with the heels of her hands, conceding it was a fair point. She slid off his lap and perched on the edge of the sofa next to him.

"Well?" Levi demanded.

She wanted to lie to him, but she didn't have the energy. "For the last few weeks, I've been battling with flashbacks of my accident, with anxiety and a range of other PTSD symptoms."

Levi stilled, his hand tightening on her thigh. "When did this start, exactly?"

Tanna pulled Ronan's jacket tightly across her body. "A couple of weeks before I left London, I attended an accident. A teenage girl was trapped, and they had to cut her out of the car."

"Just like you."

No. Wrong. He didn't understand. "Not me—she looked just like Addy. I felt like I was back there, in the car, with her. At that accident scene, I was the first person to reach the girl, but I froze. I couldn't treat her. I zoned out. My colleague had to take over." Tanna nodded, staring at the wall behind him. "Like Addy, she didn't make it. She stopped breathing and I can't help thinking if I had done something for her sooner, I could've saved her."

She hadn't admitted this, not even to herself. But Tanna knew she had to lance this wound, allow the muck to flow out. "I feel so damn guilty, Lee. About her and about Addy. Since then I've been having flash-backs, anxiety and really bad dreams, and worse than that, I second-guessed myself on the couple of res-cues I attended after that. My supervisor sent me to a psychologist, and I was put on medical leave. They strongly recommended I take a vacation and that I use the time to get therapy for my PTSD symptoms. And if I don't get it sorted out, I won't have a job."

Tanna stood up, sliding her arms into the sleeves of Ronan's jacket. She pulled in a long breath, held Levi's eyes and forced herself to speak. "I didn't fall apart just now because I had flashbacks, Levi."

"Okay." Levi frowned, puzzled. "I don't understand what you are trying to tell me, Tanna."

"I fell apart because I *didn't*," Tanna quietly stated. "I saw Sadie and I knew what I had to do, and how. I didn't think about the accident, about Addy, about that night so long ago. I just did my job."

Tanna sent him a small, sad smile. "I think I've conquered my demons, Levi."

She could go back to London, return to her job.

So why wasn't she ecstatically happy?

The next morning, Levi walked into his kitchen, crutches under his arms. Jules and Darby and Callie stood at three of the four corners of the big table, each holding a stack of different colored rectangles. The table was covered by a large piece of paper printed with circles.

The heading Lockwood–Brogan Seating Arrangements was a solid clue they were discussing his least favorite subject.

Again.

"Why does wedding planning have to take place at my house?" he demanded.

"Because Noah threatened to kidnap me and whisk me off to Vegas if I asked him one more wedding-related question," Jules told him, her attention elsewhere.

Noah was getting married and Levi was the one suffering for it? So not fair.

"Where's Tanna?" Callie asked after he gave her a kiss on her cheek. His mom looked amazing, happy and fit. Mason was good for her.

Levi didn't think he was good for Tanna.

Levi rubbed the back of his neck, thinking back to the night before. After her rock-his-world declaration, Tanna had extracted herself from his arms and headed for the restroom. When she returned, she was extraordinarily pale but dry-eyed and composed.

And as remote as a Siberian wilderness.

Instead of sleeping with him downstairs, she'd returned to the guest room and he'd given her the space she so obviously required. He'd barely slept himself, missing her soft breathing, her soft body, her gorgeous, feminine scent. He needed to see her, now. Immediately.

Crap, he was toast.

"So, what actually happened last night?" Callie asked. "I heard Tanna was involved in an emergency rescue at the Murphy cocktail party."

Levi couldn't believe how fast news traveled in Boston. And Callie, once one of Boston's most popular socialites, was still one of the first people to hear anything interesting.

Darby's head shot up. "What happened?" she asked, placing rectangles around a circle on the table.

"Carrick's new art detective choked and Tanna gave her an emergency tracheotomy," Levi told them, heading for the coffee machine. "She saved her life."

Jules's eyes widened. "That is so cool."

It was cool. But saving people had taken an enormous toll on Tanna and nobody realized the heavy burden she carried. And, as much as Tanna wanted to believe she was cured, he wasn't convinced PTSD symptoms came and went that quickly. In a few weeks, months, there might be another trigger and the symptoms could come roaring back.

He knew what she needed, and it wasn't a career

that made her relive that long ago, horrible night in all its Technicolor gruesomeness. He'd been so angry with her for so long, but he'd finally accepted and understood why she'd needed to run.

And how naive he'd been to think she was ready for marriage a few months after a serious accident, after seeing her friend die. How arrogant he'd been to think that by pulling her into marriage, pulling her under his wing, he could just make those horrible memories go away.

He'd wanted to protect her, had been so convinced marriage was the way to do that. He'd been so damn determined not to let anything bad happen to her again, to wrap her up in cotton wool, to love the memories of that night away.

But trauma couldn't be wished away, or simply forgotten or camouflaged by a white wedding and good sex. It had to be dealt with, examined, worked through, looked in the eye and wrestled with.

Tanna had been attempting to come to terms with her trauma by choosing a career where she could make a difference, to atone. To give back and lessen the survivor's guilt she lived with.

But Levi knew what she did not: guilt couldn't be assuaged by doing a job she hated.

Okay, maybe *hate* was too strong a word—a job she was good at but didn't particularly enjoy. Because her eyes didn't light up with excitement when she spoke about emergency medicine, her lips didn't curl upward like they did when she was talking about a painting or admiring the design of a dress, the intricate work that went into making Victorian-era jewelry.

He knew what she didn't: she belonged in Boston, at Murphy's, working in a field she adored, with her family. She'd blossomed since she'd come back to Boston. And her unfurling had nothing—okay, maybe a little—do with him. But any fool could see she was happy here, that Boston was where she needed to be.

Levi stared out the kitchen window, thinking hard. His agreement with Tanna, if they could still call it by that name, had only a few weeks left. Revenge was forgotten and he'd moved past the idea of a no-strings fling. He didn't have much time to persuade her not to go back to London, to start a new life, or a new chapter of her life, in Boston.

With him.

Levi pushed his phone into the back pocket of his faded jeans and stared out onto the snow-covered back garden. They were older, wiser, still crazy attracted.

They worked. Nobody else did, or ever would. She was his person and she belonged in Boston, with him.

And damn, it was time she realized that.

Levi wanted her in his house and his life. He still wanted to marry her, wanted her to be the only one to wear his ring.

His heart lurched into his throat and felt like it was stuck there. He'd tried that once before and it hadn't worked out. She'd bailed.

She wouldn't do that again, he argued with himself.

Or, if she wanted to, he was pretty sure he could talk her out of it.

They'd made no promises, but he could see their connection—it was too early, and he was too scared to call it love—in her eyes. It was in her actions, in her touch, and he sensed it when she curled up into him, pulling his arm around her to hold her close. He saw it in the way she loved to touch him—from soft, gentle, I'm-so-glad-you're-here touches to hot, greedy kisses at night.

It would be okay—it had to be. Life would never be so cruel as to give him a taste of her only to rip her from his life again.

They'd make it this time. They were stronger, wiser, older, more sensible. It would be fine…

"Levi, where do you think we should put Cousin Bob?"

Levi gripped the bridge of his nose with his thumb and index finger. "The point is, why would you invite him in the first place? He's a stepcousin once removed and we only ever see or speak to him at weddings. Or funerals."

"He's family!" Jules protested, but her eyes told him she was willing to be convinced.

"If you invite him, you're asking for trouble."

Jules nodded. She crumpled the rectangle and tossed it at Levi's chest. "Cousin Bob will not receive his formal invitation. That okay with you, Mom?"

"Since the man tried to French kiss me on my wedding day, I'm more than okay with it." Callie smiled, her eyes far away. "Your dad punched him, sent him flying into the cake."

His sisters' mouths fell open and Levi laughed.

"I've seen pictures of your cake. It was beautiful," Jules wailed.

"And it tasted like sawdust. All of Aunt Penelope's cakes did. She was brilliant at icing, but her cakes were revolting," Callie explained. "I wasn't upset."

Weddings, Levi thought. He couldn't wait for this one to be over. But, as soon as it was done, he'd have to listen to DJ's plans, then Darby's. Why was life punishing him like this? And why in his own house?

"Morning."

Levi's head spun around to see Tanna across the room, standing in the doorway, dressed in jeans, boots and her thigh-length leather coat. With a multicolored scarf wrapped around her throat, she looked like she was heading out.

She probably wanted some air, Levi told himself. Maybe she thought they needed supplies—he had to be misreading the *I'm leaving* sign flashing in her eyes.

He was overreacting...

He hoped.

Tanna answered the few questions his nosy sisters threw at her about last night's excitement, her answers becoming more clipped as the discussion progressed. Yeah, she was still upset by Sadie's choking incident and she didn't want to rehash it.

Tanna stepped into the kitchen and put her hands into the pockets of her coat. It was warm in the kitchen. In a second, she'd slip it off, head for the coffee machine, slide into a chair.

Tanna just looked down at the large sheet, her expression curious. "Are you trying to torture Levi with wedding plans?"

He was pretty sure that was their intention. "I don't have any room at Lockwood House," Jules replied.

Yeah sure, he wasn't buying what she was selling. Jules lived at Noah's family estate, Lockwood House, the first house in the country-club community, and still magnificent. Callie and Darby, beneficiaries of the Brogan Family Trust, lived in houses just as big.

"BS," he said.

Jules exchanged a look with Callie and gently shrugged. "Being here makes me feel closer to Dad. It's as if I'm waiting for him to come in from work, just hanging like we used to do. He'd be so involved in the planning, driving me nuts—"

Levi stared down at his coffee cup, wishing he could ignore the jealousy he always experienced when he heard the sad, wistful, loving note in his sisters' voices when they spoke of their father.

His relationship with his father had been so different from the twins'. With them their dad had been softer, more relaxed, kinder. They hadn't seen the extremes of his personality, his drive and his reckless need to push the boundaries.

They had no idea their father took so many risks, that he flew so close to the sun.

Why was Levi so different from Ray? Why did he need to have everything tied up, corralled and controlled? Why did he feel the need to restrain his dad's actions, have this fierce need to protect his mom and sisters? Where had that come from and why was he like that?

He'd always thought it was because his dad took too many business risks, but Levi had been anxious long before he became aware of his dad's business practices.

What had happened to make him feel this way?

Well, huh, so Tanna wasn't the only one who had unresolved issues from her past.

Tanna's shoulder pushed into his biceps and then her hand came to rest between his shoulder blades, her touch reassuring. Suddenly everything inside him stilled and his resentment and guilt retreated as her touch filled him.

He didn't need to be in control; he didn't need to have his life wrapped up in a box, tied with a bow. He didn't need much—hell, he didn't need anything—if Tanna stood next to him, in his house and in his life.

He needed her. Period.

"Are your brothers bringing guests to the wedding?" Jules asked Tanna, her question pulling Levi from his thoughts.

"Ah, that's not something they'd share with me," Tanna replied, sounding apologetic. "But yeah, I guess they would."

"Okay, so do you and Levi want to sit with us or with them?"

Levi started to tell Jules it really didn't matter, but then he looked down at Tanna and saw guilt infuse her face. He frowned, and panic squeezed his lungs, tightening his throat.

Jules looked from the seating plan to them, her brow furrowed. "Well?"

Tanna bit her lip and her eyes clouded over. Levi's stomach hit the floor and bounced.

Don't do it, Tan. Don't say it.

Don't break my heart again.

For God's sake, don't run.

"Can I get back to you on that?" Tanna replied, her smile forced.

Levi wanted to feel relieved at not hearing the words he knew would change everything, but he couldn't. There was too much happening in Tanna's lovely eyes for him to feel comfortable. Or reassured.

Tanna forced a smile onto her lips and excused herself. Levi frowned, grabbed his crutches and followed her out of the kitchen.

Something was going on here and he wanted to know what the hell it was.

Twelve

Saving Sadie had been a sign from the universe, Tanna decided, walking out of the kitchen.

It was life's way of telling her that emergency medicine was what she was supposed to be doing, how she was meant to operate in the world. That Levi—and a life spent with him, working at Murphy's—wasn't something she could seriously consider, or consider at all.

And maybe she'd needed to come back to Boston to be reminded of that.

She'd grown up surrounded by amazing pieces of art, her childhood home in Beacon Hill was better than most museums. She'd been taught to appreciate the stroke of a paintbrush, a perfectly constructed dovetail joint, the fine placement of micro mosaics, the impact of negative space. She'd come to revere the Old Masters, to interrogate the meaning behind abstract paintings, to look beyond the surface.

Her family made their living from trading beautiful objects, from passing pieces of wondrous art from one collector to another.

But, when faced with death, their bodies battered and broken, people didn't think of Monet's *Water Lilies* or Fabergé's brilliantly constructed, jewel-encrusted golden eggs. Thoughts about furniture made in rosewood or bronze sculptures didn't happen.

Tanna would bet her trust fund Sadie had been more concerned with survival, in taking the next breath, in getting through the next second, the next minute, the next hour than she had been about those fantastic dresses she'd been admiring earlier.

People who were badly injured needed to fight and they needed a chance. Tanna's job, her training, helped them do that.

It was important. It was necessary. It was what she was supposed to do.

Tanna stood in front of the massive windows in the most formal of Levi's sitting rooms and ignored the richly decorated room behind her. If she stayed in Boston, if she continued to live with Levi, she'd slide back into being a Murphy, into the society princess she'd been before. Levi might not be as extroverted or as sociable as his father but he was still a Brogan, still one of the most prominent men in Boston.

And as a Murphy, she was a Boston princess, and if she stayed, she'd be expected to fill that role. If she joined the PR department of Murphy's then attending the social events of rich East Coasters, wearing designer clothes and shoes, would be part of her job.

How could she stand around talking art when she knew she should be out there saving someone's life? How could she live with herself? Within weeks, months, she'd be discontented; within a year she'd loathe herself. Why put herself through that?

And how would Addy feel, knowing she'd sacrificed her life so Tanna could be a woman who stood around drinking champagne, eating canapés and talking through the finer points of a painting with collectors who were wealthy enough to buy a small third world country?

Addy would be disappointed in Tanna and her actions would confirm all Addy's mother's accusations— she would be just another rich girl, her life sprinkled with fairy dust, unable to live in the real world and do a tough job.

The bottom line: Tanna hadn't cheated death to waste her life and her education. Yeah, she'd had a tough time in the hospital after her accident, but she hadn't suffered, not really. She was still alive, wasn't she?

She wasn't unhappy in London. She could cope. Okay, leaving Levi, not waking up with him, sharing his bed and his body, not being able to kick back and relax in his wonderful home, laughing and loving him, would be tough. But she'd left him before and, like back then, leaving Levi was necessary.

Besides, unlike before, this time her leaving wouldn't

hurt him. He'd told her, without equivocation, that he'd never trust her with his heart again, that he'd never allow himself to love her again, so while he might miss the sex, he wouldn't miss her.

Her leaving wouldn't break his heart.

It might well break hers.

But she'd still leave.

She had to.

Levi found her in the formal sitting room, the one with the portrait of his father over the fireplace and a Picasso sketch on the wall between the two arched windows. He didn't come into this room often as this was the "formal" room, the one the family used for serious conversations.

These walls had heard more than a few of his discussions—or fights—with his dad. In this room he'd told his folks he banged up his brand-new car, and the walls had been witness to the many fights with Ray over deals Levi thought were too risky, and to Ray losing his temper when Levi told him he was leaving Brogan LLC.

Few conversations in this room had ended well.

He was pretty sure this one wouldn't either.

Tanna stood by the left window, her arms crossed tightly against her chest, staring out the window at the snow falling outside.

Winter in Boston. Cold enough to freeze the balls off any primate.

"Want to tell me what's going on?" Levi placed his

crutches against the back of the sofa. He bit the bullet. "Why didn't you answer Jules's simple question?"

When he received nothing from her but heavy silence, his irritation started to build. "What's going on, Tanna?"

Tanna finally turned around. "You know why I didn't answer her question, Levi. I'm not going to be around for her wedding."

And there it was, confirmation of his biggest fear.

She was leaving him, again.

"So, you're still planning on going back to London in a few weeks?"

"No."

His heart soared, she was staying...

"I'm leaving today, flying out tonight. I called them and told them I was coming back."

Levi felt his battered heart, and all his organs, plunge back down to earth.

You're not going to die, Brogan. It just feels like it.

Levi swallowed and rubbed his hand over his face. "Is that a wise decision? How do you know you won't have an attack tomorrow, or next week?"

"Thanks for the vote of confidence," Tanna retorted before lifting and dropping her hands in obvious frustration. "Admittedly, I can't guarantee the panic attacks and the anxiety won't come back, Levi."

She continued to speak. "But they didn't affect me while I was working on Sadie. The tracheotomy was a scary, serious option and I handled myself. That's a huge improvement. I called my supervisor today, told him what happened, and he was impressed. He agreed

I could come back on a trial basis, that I still have to go for therapy but if I don't have another attack on the job over the next month, I'll be fully reinstated."

"And what happens if any of your PTSD symptoms return?"

"As long as they don't affect my job, I'll deal."

He didn't want her to deal, he wanted her to be happy. Levi opened his mouth, ready to persuade her to stay. He'd start by telling her Carrick would employ her tomorrow, that she was both needed and wanted at Murphy's.

At the cocktail party, he'd seen the joy in her eyes as she spoke about art, how she loved interacting with their clients, charming both old and new customers alike. He'd listened to her long conversation with Jane about publicity for an upcoming sale of rubies, spinels and red sapphires. They'd been talking about how to publicize the "Red" sale and Tanna had been fully engaged in the conversation, her creative mind running fast and happy.

He knew she'd be so much happier in Boston, working at Murphy's, than in London, providing emergency medicine. But what did that help if Tanna believed differently?

He had to make her understand. "Why do you feel the need to go back, Tanna?"

Tanna shook her head. "I need to be out there, doing something important, playing my part."

Levi sighed. "At what cost, Tanna? How can I let you go back to London, knowing that the PTSD might come back and worrying about you being alone and in a strange place?"

"How can you let me?" Tanna's voice dropped a couple of degrees. "You don't *let* me do a damn thing, Brogan. And London is more my home than Boston."

Bad choice of words. Levi swallowed down his desire to howl. "Why can't you see that your place is here, that Boston is where you are supposed to be? It's so damn obvious. I'm trying to understand why you are being so stubborn, so determined to leave me, to leave Boston again. Work with me here."

Tanna's eyes shot green fire. "My place? Are you kidding me?"

Brilliant time to use misogynistic words, Brogan. You idiot. Maybe he should just keep his mouth shut. But then she'd definitely leave...

And that was unacceptable.

"We'll come back to your crazy notion that you still think you have some sort of power over what I do with my life..." Tanna told him, her face taut with tension. "I'm not leaving, Levi. I never came back."

Okay, then.

"I'm good at my job, Levi. Or didn't you notice I saved someone's life last night?"

"I was there," Levi said, trying hard not to sound snappish. "I also held you as you dissolved in my arms. Do you think I like seeing that happen?"

"Do you think I like having it happen?" Tanna shot back. "What's important is that I didn't freeze or have an anxiety attack. That's *all* that's important."

"Not to me. Your happiness is important. Doing something you love, every day, is important."

Loving me is important.

"It's the price I pay, Levi, for the life I've had, the life I *have*."

Say what? What the hell did she mean?

Levi walked over to her and turned her so she faced him, her eyes defiant. "No, you don't get to brush me off without an explanation. Talk to me, Tanna. What did you mean by that last statement?"

"Can you please leave it alone, Brogan?"

Not this time. Tanna had been left alone for far too long. "Explain."

"Dammit." Tanna pushed her hair back from her face before unwinding her scarf from around her neck.

"Take off your coat," Levi told her. "You're not going anywhere until we thrash this out."

Wrong move because Tanna just narrowed her eyes at his barked order. "I'm not staying long enough to do that. Do you want to hear this or do you want to nag me?"

Keep it together, Brogan. You're not doing yourself any favors.

Levi tightened his lips and gestured for her to continue.

"Before my accident, I lived a charmed life—you can't deny it."

"You did lose your parents when you were a toddler."

"But I had my brothers who adored me. I was wealthy and protected, spoiled beyond belief."

Levi thought she was exaggerating but at this point he was picking his battles.

"Then I had a brutal accident, but I came through it, thanks to having access to some of the best doctors in the country. I even ended up falling in love with a handsome, rich guy who wanted to marry me."

This was a problem?

"Isla, Addy's mom, called me Little Miss Lucky. She said I lived a charmed life and that I had no idea what reality looked like."

"When did she say that to you and why am I only hearing about this now?" Levi demanded, furious.

"When I left the hospital, I went to visit her. She was not happy to see me. She basically told me I should've died, not Addy."

Levi's temper spiked and he reminded himself the woman had lost her only child. "She was grieving. People say things they don't mean when they are in pain."

Tanna tried to smile. "I saw her recently too, the same day I barged in here, actually. She hasn't changed her opinion."

Levi desperately wanted to hold her. "I'm sorry, Tan."

Tanna tried to look nonchalant but didn't quite get there. Isla's opinions still affected her. "I also overheard quite a few conversations between the nurses, some I'm pretty sure they meant for me to hear. Some of it was nasty, but a lot of what they said was true."

"Like?" Levi demanded.

"I was rich and spoiled and had no idea what it felt like to live in a world that frequently isn't kind and is definitely unfair. After all, only a girl sprinkled with fairy dust could survive a near-fatal car accident and then, during convalescence, find herself a handsome fiancé, making plans to go back to college to finish her degree while he supported her and then work at a cushy job in the family company when she was done studying."

"Sounds like jealousy to me. Why are we discussing this?"

"Because those women poured water on the seeds of discontent I was already feeling. I did feel useless, unsure of who I was and what I was doing. But mostly I felt so damn guilty about being alive. About continuing to live my charmed life when Addy was dead. I felt this urge to do more, to be more."

"And you couldn't do that, in Boston, with me?"

Tanna shook her head. "If I'd stayed, I'd always be your wife, the spoiled and pampered princess. I needed to leave, Levi. I needed—need—to do what Addy couldn't. I need to make a difference."

"You always were more, Tanna," Levi said, his voice growly from all the emotion he was trying to suppress. "You were the one who decided you were going to walk again, the one who refused to give up and give in. You proved everyone wrong. You have no idea how strong you are. And I, for one, am profoundly grateful you didn't die back then, Tanna."

Tanna lifted her fingers to her mouth, her eyes bright with unshed tears. He knew this conversation was hurting her but they needed to talk this through. She needed to understand. "I read somewhere one of the hardest things in life is to let go. Guilt, anger, love, loss, betrayal, it becomes a habit to hold on to it, and it's tough to let it go."

Levi lifted his hand to hold her cheek. "You need to let it go, Tanna."

Tanna stepped back and held up her hands, trying to put a barrier between them. "I need to let it go? That's rich coming from you, Levi."

Levi frowned, not understanding her.

"When are you going to stop trying to control everything because you couldn't control your dad?"

There were talking about her, not him. He was fine. Well, mostly fine. And his relationship with his dad had nothing to do with her, and his feelings for her.

But, if it helped to move this conversation along, to get the result he wanted, he'd make a tiny concession. "We're both carrying baggage from our past, Tanna, but I'm not the one who is walking away, *again*."

Tanna glared, her jaw tight with tension. "What does that even mean, Levi? Are you telling me you want to start something with me?"

Levi shook his head. "Honey, we don't need to start a damn thing because we never ended it. I'm as crazy about you as I ever was."

Tanna stared at him, shocked. "Please! If you really mean what you are saying, come back to London with me, live in my small apartment, support me as I do my job."

Levi made sure his look was steady, that she saw his determination. "I could agree to that, and I would do that, in a heartbeat. But—"

"And here comes the but!" Tanna mocked him.

God, keeping his temper was killing him.

This would be so much easier if he just tossed her over his shoulder and locked her in his room, naked, until she came to her senses.

"But I don't think my moving to London would solve the problem because you would still be unhappy. You've been unhappy for a long, long time."

"And you think my moving back to Boston would resolve that issue?"

Of course it would! Why couldn't she see it? What was wrong with her? And what was wrong with him that he couldn't make her see something that was so damn obvious?

This was like arguing with his dad all over again.

"It sure as hell couldn't hurt," he muttered.

Levi tried to rein in his impatience and tried to even out his voice. "If I knew you loved your job, that it excited you, that it energized you, I could understand your wanting to return to London. But you don't. You're just going through the motions, trying to assuage your guilt, to make amends for something that wasn't your fault."

"She died, Levi! Because I was drunk and asked her to drive."

He heard the panic in her voice and shook his head. "She died because it was an accident, sweetheart. A horrible accident. Please stop punishing yourself."

Levi jammed his bunched fists into the pockets of his track pants. Although he already knew what her answer would be, he knew he had to ask. Just once.

"Don't go, Tanna. Stay here, with me."

Tanna didn't reply but her silence was answer enough.

He'd argued his position, tried to make her see the situation from his perspective, had been forceful in his opinions. But Tanna had held her position, she hadn't moved an inch.

He'd failed to control the rapidly deteriorating situation...

She was running away, again. From him, today. And he had to let her.

He had to let her leave. The thought hit him with the impact of a punch to his heart and, feeling a little unsteady, he locked his knees.

He knew that keeping her here—even if he could do that, and he couldn't—wasn't fair to either of them. She had to figure this out herself.

He wanted to be her choice; he wanted to be her person. She was his, she always had been, but he was an all-or-nothing type of guy; he didn't want to live with doubt—hers, his, theirs.

He had to let her go.

She'd run the last time, but this time he needed to respect her enough, love her enough, to stop trying to control her.

He'd lived without her once, he could do it again. How, he didn't have the smallest clue, but he would. What other choice did he have?

Levi stared down at the hardwood floors beneath his feet and gathered his courage, prepared to give Tanna the one thing she needed the most, unconditional acceptance, tangible support.

"Tan, baby, look at me."

Levi waited until her tearstained eyes met his and he fought the urge to sweep her into his arms, to love all that pain away.

But he couldn't, not this time. "Tan…go."

Tanna jerked back and her sexy mouth fell open in complete shock. "What did you say?"

Levi knew she'd heard him. "Go back to London, Tan."

"But…I thought…you… Crap." Tanna threw up her hands, obviously frustrated. "I thought you wanted me to stay in Boston, for us to be together?"

He did, as much as he wanted his heart to keep pumping. "You know I do, but I don't want you here if that's not what you want too. I only want you in Boston, back with me, if there's nowhere else you want to be, nothing else you want to do."

"I'll always want to work, Levi."

She wasn't understanding him. "I don't care what you do for work. I just care whether you love it. Whether doing it every day makes you happy. Don't you understand that your happiness is all I care about?" Levi sucked in some air and forced himself to smile. "I'd rather you be in London, doing whatever the hell you want, than being miserable with me, Tan."

"Lee…"

No, damn, he was done here. He couldn't do this anymore, he was done with being strong. She needed to leave…

So did he.

Levi stepped forward, dropped a kiss on Tanna's

temple and rubbed his thumb, just once more, over her full bottom lip. "For God's sake, be happy, Tan. That's all I've ever wanted for you."

Levi picked up his crutches, jammed them under his arms and headed for the door.

Levi sat on the expensive leather sofa facing his father's portrait, needing to be in the room where he'd last seen Tanna.

Sometimes he closed his eyes and imagined her standing by the window, the weak winter sun turning her hair the color of a raven's wing. He could still see her perfect profile, smell her subtle perfume.

She was in his thoughts, his dreams, the place his mind went to every minute of the day.

He more than missed her—he craved her, longed for her. Hell, why not just be pathetic and admit that he was pining for her? It was like she'd sucked every shade of color from his life...

Melodramatic much, Brogan?

If he didn't pull himself together, he'd soon find himself reading *Romeo and Juliet* and watching those cry-me-a-river breakup movies.

Levi heard the door open behind him and didn't bother to look around. It would either be his mother or one of his annoying sisters, none of whom he wanted to see. If he couldn't be with Tanna then he just wanted to be alone.

Yep, definitely pathetic.

Levi looked at his father's portrait and ignored his

mom sitting down next to him, shoulder to shoulder, thigh to thigh. Levi felt her concerned eyes on his face.

"I'm *fine*, Mom."

"Physically maybe," Callie conceded. "Your shoulder is healed, and you can move around without pain. Your body heals quickly, Lee."

He knew she was waiting for him to respond, but because he was both stubborn and obstinate, he didn't. He'd bet the contents of his bank account that his mom had more to say. And she would—she didn't need any encouragement from him.

"Your heart takes forever to heal."

Yep, there it was. His mom was trying to get into his head. He was almost too tired, too heartsick to care. "Whatever, Mom."

Callie poked him in the thigh with a rather sharp nail. "Don't you *whatever* me, Levi Ray Brogan."

Callie folded her arms and out of the corner of his eye, he saw her looking at his father's portrait. "Your dad. God, he drove me nuts."

Levi frowned at the hint of annoyance he heard in her voice. He wasn't going to ask, he really wasn't…

Luckily Callie offered an explanation before his pride took a beating. "Your dad was this big, bright, bold force of energy who loved to be loved. And I did love him, Levi."

Levi turned to look at Callie and, seeing her distress, rested his big hand on her knee. "I've never had any doubt about that, Mom. You grieved him for a long time."

Callie nodded. "I did. But when he died, I also grieved the person I was, the person I could've been."

Levi half turned, putting his shoulder into the back of the couch. "I don't understand…"

Callie's smile was soft. "One of the reasons Mason and I took some time to come together was because I didn't know who I was without your dad—there'd never been a me without him. I didn't know if I could be me, without Ray."

"Yet, I could only ever be me. I couldn't be the person he wanted me to be," Levi murmured.

Callie threaded her fingers through his, her eyes sad. "He'd agree his greatest failing was you, Lee. All our fights were always about you."

He'd not known that, and it added another layer of guilt to the heavy load he carried. "I'm sorry, Mom."

Callie's grip on his hand tightened. "Oh, no, that was on your dad, not you. You didn't do anything wrong."

"I was so mad at him, so often. I hated the risks he took, his lack of control. I hated him worrying you, putting everything we had at risk. He's been dead for a long time but I'm still so angry that I couldn't get through to him, that he was so damn impulsive and impetuous."

"But that's not the only reason why you're angry with him," Callie said, her voice low and sad.

"I'm pretty sure that it is, Mom."

Callie turned to face him, her beautiful face tight with tension. "You never forgave your father for nearly killing you all by driving too fast and spinning out."

Levi stared at her, conscious his heart was in his

throat and his stomach was tying itself up in knots. He swallowed but his throat didn't clear so he swallowed again.

"I don't know what you are talking about, Mom."

"Yes, you do, Lee."

It was a memory he'd pushed down deep, something he, very deliberately, chose not to remember. He had been young, five or six, and he remembered the music blaring, the huge smiles on the twins' faces and his dad flinging them around the sharp corners of a long forgotten road, speeding up every time the twins yelled for him to go faster. Levi had screamed at Ray to slow down, begging him to brake and yelling repeatedly that they were going to crash.

His father had mocked him for being a scaredy-cat and told him that his sisters had more guts than he did. His sisters had been too young to realize the danger they were in.

Then Ray lost control of his car and Levi remembered them spinning and spinning and spinning...

Levi scrubbed his hands over his face, recalling the dust, the sharp whine of the car scraping along the barrier, the twins' soft sobs and his father's white face. The long drop below them when they finally, finally came to a standstill.

Ray begged Levi not to tell Callie and he stopped trusting his father that day.

"He nearly killed us, Mom. It was so damn close." Levi croaked the words out. "He said I shouldn't tell you, that it would upset you terribly. After all, we were all fine."

Callie shook her head. "Your father couldn't live with himself and he did tell me, about three months after it happened. I was so mad at him and we didn't talk for weeks, months." Callie rested her forehead on his shoulder. "That's why you are so protective of the twins, why you never, really, trusted your father's decisions, about anything, again."

Her statement made sense. His lack of trust in his dad had been born that afternoon.

"Every time he took a risk, I think I was subliminally reminded of that summer afternoon and I hated him for it," Levi admitted. "And maybe I overreacted at some of the things he did—maybe they weren't as bad as I thought."

"Oh, most were," Callie admitted. "Risk-taking was his nature, Lee. Nothing you did or said would've changed him."

Callie leaned into him, her head on the ball of his shoulder. "For what it's worth and no matter what you think, he was extraordinarily proud of you, Lee."

Levi rested his head on his mother's. "That's good to know, Mom."

"But it's not what's keeping you up at night, right?"

Levi managed to smile. "No, it's not." He shrugged, looking past Callie's sympathetic face to the wet, miserable day beyond the window. "I miss her."

"You never stopped missing her, Lee. And I don't think your heart was healed from the last time she left. Hearts as big as yours don't heal quickly."

Yeah, not what he needed to hear. Levi slid down

the sofa and rested his head on the back. "I let her go, Mom. No, I *told* her to go."

Callie was silent for a minute, maybe more. "I think it's amazingly brave of you, Levi. Because staying, or going, has to be her choice," Callie replied. "You can't force love, Levi. You know that better than most. You deserve to be loved completely, unreservedly."

Levi nodded. "But it still hurts like hell." Levi took a deep breath, knowing he could tell Callie this, that she was the one person who'd understand.

"Just for once, Mom, I want to be the person Tanna runs back to, not away from."

Thirteen

Carrick stood in the private viewing space overlooking the sale floor and watched Ronan work the room. His brother, their chief auctioneer, hadn't planned on running this vintage clothing auction but, thanks to Tanna, many of Raeni's old contacts and clients were present and all had expressed the wish to see a Murphy controlling the sale.

Their wishes were his command so his charming, fast-talking brother did what he did best: push up prices with wit and laughter and natural charm.

Carrick lifted his eyebrows when a dress hit the fifty thousand mark and shook his head. God, Tanna would've loved this; she would've been out on the floor, spotting bids or working a phone for a client who couldn't be present. Either way, she would've loved to have been part of the evening.

But Tanna was back in London and Levi wasn't answering his calls so Carrick could only presume they'd messed up their second chance.

Would any Murphy sibling ever find love?

Carrick was divorced from Satan's bride, Ronan's wife, Thandi, had died giving birth to Aron, his second son, and who the hell knew why Finn and Beah had gotten divorced?

He'd had high hopes for Tanna and Levi, but his sister's rapid departure back to London suggested their relationship had hit the rocks…again.

Carrick leaned into the wall as Ronan banged his gavel down, indicating the dress was sold. Next up was a vintage Hermès handbag, an item Carrick knew many of the buyers had expressed interest in. Although he was separated from his well-dressed and very loaded clients by a glass window, he could feel the energy in the room change. He'd been doing this long enough to know a bidding war was about to break out and he smiled; bidding wars were spectacularly good for the Murphy International bank account.

Carrick scanned the room, his eyes bouncing over perfectly made-up faces, coiffed hair, stupendous jewelry. He identified a few of his clients and smiled at Frieda Talbot, sporting a necklace of matched pearls the size of marbles and a don't-mess-with-my-checkbook look.

Along the sides of the room his staff manned the phones and standing to the right of them was a blonde in a rich blue-and-black-patterned wraparound dress and wearing high-heeled boots.

Sadie.

Carrick's heart kicked up and he drank in her features, smiling at the excitement on her face. A small smile played about her lips and her eyes flipped between the big screen on the wall, showing a picture of the next item up for sale, to the bidders in the room. There was a supermodel and a famous dress designer and an A-list Hollywood actress, so maybe she was a little starstruck.

Sadie lifted her hand to her throat and he remembered her doing that the other night as he slid inside her, warm and wet and wonderful.

He'd headed over to Sadie's apartment to see whether she'd recovered from her brief hospital visit but when he knocked on her door, a huge bunch of flowers in hand, she'd grabbed his tie and pulled him into her home and locked her lips on his.

Clothes started flying soon afterward and he'd ended up making love to her for most of the night.

The next morning, they'd both agreed it was a one-time thing…

But looking at her standing there, excitement in her eyes, he wanted her again.

But he'd mixed business and pleasure before and it had blown up in his face.

He'd be stupid to do that again.

But, hell, if he was given the opportunity to be stupid again, in that particular way, he'd jump at the chance.

* * *

In her fabulous and luxurious apartment in Marble Arch, Padma dumped a healthy amount of red wine into Tanna's silver goblet and pushed it across the marble kitchen counter that hadn't seen a pot, or a homemade meal, since 1992.

Padma had an arrangement with several Michelin star chefs in London that, if she didn't eat at one of their restaurants, they delivered. Padma—with her dark eyes, scarlet lipstick and complete self-confidence—had no problem bending egotistic head chefs and restaurant owners to her way of thinking.

That amount of self-possession both impressed and terrified Tanna.

"So, how was your first week back at work?" Padma demanded, perching on a bar stool on the other side of the counter and lighting up a cigarette.

Tanna shrugged. "Cold. Wet. Quiet, mostly. We did a couple of training exercises yesterday."

Tanna took a sip of her wine and ran her hand over her hair, pulled back into a tight braid. London was London; nothing much had changed in a month.

Although it did feel like she'd rocketed back a decade as her thoughts were consumed by Levi.

Was he okay? How was his leg? Was he missing her? Furious with her? She hadn't heard anything from him since she left ten days ago and she kept checking her phone, desperate to hear something.

But nope, nothing.

Tanna sighed, ripped the band from her braid and raked her fingers through her hair, wincing as her scalp tingled. If she were with Levi, she'd ask him to massage her scalp and he would, then his hands would move to her neck and her back, his fingers digging into her knots. But within a couple of minutes he'd become distracted and his hands would wander to her breast, between her legs...

Tanna blinked when Padma flicked her hand with a glossy, red-tipped finger. "Earth to Tanna."

Tanna ran the tip of her finger around the rim of her goblet. She couldn't help thinking about Levi. She missed him as much as she would an amputated limb. Had she done the right thing leaving?

She'd thought that when she touched down in London, she'd feel better about her decision to leave Boston, but it never happened. She'd thought she'd feel settled when she walked through the door to her Wimbledon apartment, but...nope.

On the first day back at work, at the end of the first week...

Nothing. Ten days later she was still questioning her decision, was still wondering if leaving Boston was the right thing to do.

"Have you responded to any emergency calls this week?" Padma asked.

Tanna nodded. "A car accident on the A3 the day before yesterday, a bomb threat at a politician's office."

Padma's expression turned speculative and Tanna knew what was coming next. "And how are you?"

"I'm fine, fairy godmother."

Padma's thin fingers encircled her wrist and she

squeezed to get Tanna's attention. "Tanna, this is me. Tell me."

Tanna rubbed the back of her neck. "I've actually been fine," she admitted. "I thought the multicar pileup would be a trigger and I kept waiting for the anxiety to strike but nothing. Not when I was treating patients or later, when I was alone at home."

"Nothing at all?" Padma asked, her thin, perfectly penciled eyebrows flying upward.

She sounded like Tanna's supervisor, who kept taking her emotional temperature, constantly hovering. "Absolutely nothing. I think it's gone as quickly as it arrived."

"So, if the trigger was the accident where the young girl died, what made the PTSD symptoms disappear?"

Tanna was scared to call herself cured; she was asking for trouble if she did that. But maybe she had the symptoms under control.

Tanna thought about how to answer Padma's question. "I think it was doing that tracheotomy. I was terrified but I did it. I cried all over Levi afterward but I think I cried it all out."

Padma sipped her wine before rolling the bowl between the palms of her hands. "Ah, you've finally mentioned Levi. I was wondering when you were going to pull him into the conversation."

Tanna undid the zip on her work coveralls to reveal the black T-shirt underneath. Was Padma preparing to sweat the truth out of her? "Can we turn the heat down?"

"No," Padma replied, putting her wine down. "It's not hot. You're just feeling uncomfortable."

"Anyone would be when faced with your tell-me-everything expression," Tanna shot back.

There wasn't a boundary Padma wouldn't cross, so Tanna waited for the third, or thirty-third, degree. Instead of throwing questions at her, Padma lit up another cigarette and, through the smoke, squinted at Tanna. "Do you love him?"

Of course she did. "I never stopped loving him."

"Uh-huh." Padma inhaled then picked up her wine again. Before taking a sip, she waved the goblet back and forth. "So, that being established, can I ask why you are in my apartment, in London, drinking my wine when you could be with him having great sex?"

It was a question Tanna asked herself often. "My job is here, Padma."

"They don't need medical people in Boston?"

"No, I mean, yes, of course they do," Tanna replied, flustered.

"So, you could be in Boston, with Levi, doing what you do now," Padma said prosaically. She narrowed her eyes and leaned forward. "Let's try that again... Why aren't you in Boston, with the man you say you love?"

Tanna could lie, spin her a line, but she was tired of lying to herself, and to others. "Because I'm scared."

"You should be scared. Love is scary." Padma shrugged, unfazed. "But what, specifically, are you scared of?"

"I don't want to hurt him again," Tanna fudged.

Padma sent her a hard-eyed squint, worthy of one

of *Macbeth*'s witches. "Be honest with yourself, Tanna Murphy."

Tanna blew air into her cheeks. "How can I ask for more when I've already had, have, so much, Padma? When I'm alive, breathing, living, for God's sake!"

There it was, in black-and-white.

The crux of what she was feeling. She was fit and healthy and wealthy. Did she have a right to love and happiness, as well? She had her brothers and her trust fund and the means to go anywhere and do anything.

Addy never had the opportunity to live a fraction of the life Tanna had. Who was she to expect or want marriage and babies and great sex when Addy didn't get to experience any of that?

When Tanna finished her bumbling explanation, Padma leaned back in her chair and folded her arms across her Armani silk shirt. Ignoring both her burning cigarette and her wine, Padma pursed her lips. Tanna, who thought she knew Padma well, couldn't decipher her expression.

Whatever Padma was thinking, Tanna hoped she treated her gently. Her heart was split wide-open, her belly exposed, and vulnerability pumped from every pore.

Padma opened her mouth to speak, snapped it closed and shook her head. Hopping off the stool, she paced the area between the island and the kitchen counters, scowling at the expensive marble floor.

Padma, the most languid woman Tanna had ever met, was expending energy. And that meant she was either upset or...pissed.

"What a lot of horse crap."

Pissed it was, then.

Maybe Padma wasn't the person Tanna should be sharing her inner fears with. Then again, she was one person—apart from Levi—Tanna could trust to give it to her straight.

"I have a question for you…"

Tanna nodded and reached for her wine. This conversation most definitely needed the soothing powers of expensive alcohol.

"Please explain how your living small, not having a relationship, not touching your trust fund has helped Addy."

This again?

"I've helped a lot of people, Padma. I've saved a few lives. I learned how to budget, to live within my salary, the difference between wants and needs. I think I've grown up."

Padma stopped pacing and her dark eyes pinned Tanna to her seat. "Maybe. But you didn't answer the question… How does any of that, how does staying here in London and not being with Levi, help Addy?"

Was this a trick question? "It doesn't. She's dead."

"So, why are you sacrificing yourself, sacrificing your happiness for a dead person? Is that something she'd expect you to do?"

Tanna swirled her wine around in her glass. "Her mom was so mad, Padma. So angry I survived, and Addy didn't. To her, it was just another example of the rich getting everything they wanted and the poor getting the bad deal."

Padma winced. "The woman lost her only child, Tanna. But that's her perception, not yours. You can't make your life smaller, deny yourself happiness because Addy died. In fact, many people would say you should honor her memory by living the best life you can. You've paid back any debt you think you owe, Tanna."

Padma took both Tanna's hands in hers and squeezed. "Nobody is going to forgive you, Tanna. No one is going to say it is okay, to tell you that you are allowed to be happy. No one is going to give you permission to fall in love, to get married, to have babies. No one is going to rescue you from yourself, fight these demons for you, pull you out of this rut of self-flagellation. You've got to forgive your nineteen-year-old self. You've got to accept you made a decision not to drink and drive and you've got to start believing it was the only decision you could've made at the time. Denying yourself happiness is just you punishing yourself."

"I—" Tanna didn't know what to say, how to process what she was hearing.

Padma wouldn't release her grip on Tanna's hands. "Do you want to stay in London?"

Tanna touched her tongue to her top lip. "No."

"Do you still want to work in emergency medicine?"

"No, I want to work at Murphy's, but it's so damn frivolous, Pad. It's not important."

Padma released an irritated sigh. "Picasso said the purpose of art is to wash the daily dust of life off our souls."

Tanna lifted her eyebrows at her godmother, not at

the quote but at the familiarity of her use of the artist's name. "You make it sound like you knew him."

"I met him a few times in the early seventies. He was old, I was young. He thought I was beautiful, and I was... Anyway, I'm not going to let you distract me with tales of my wild youth."

And Tanna knew Padma had taken the concept of *wild* to new heights.

"Art...art is important, Tanna. The appreciation of beauty, the creation of beauty, is what makes us human. It makes us look inside ourselves, see the world from different perspectives, challenges us to think deeper. You're allowed to love what you do, darling."

Tann shook her head. "I don't want to go back to being a pampered princess, Padma."

Padma smiled at her. "Darling, you were a princess at nineteen. At nearly thirty, you are now a queen. You have fought battles, gone to war, lived and laughed and wept."

Padma lifted her fingers to push a curl off Tanna's forehead. "Baby girl, you are more than just a queen, you are a warrior queen! Now, straighten your crown and embrace your life, embrace love and be happy for God's sake!"

Tanna really wanted to, but denying herself was a hard habit to break. "I don't know how to do that, Pad."

"Well, I suggest you learn," Padma tartly replied.

A few more weeks and his cast would come off. He couldn't wait.

Levi rolled the elastic band holding the plastic cast

sleeve down his thigh and over his cast, taking the cover with it. He hadn't wanted to repeat the duct tape experiment and lose more of his leg hair, so Tanna had suggested the rubber bands and they worked like a dream, allowing him to shower without getting his cast wet.

Levi wrapped a towel around his waist and pushed his dripping hair off his face. Gripping the edges of the basin, he looked up into the mirror and grimaced at his pale face and the strips of blue under his eyes.

He'd been pushing himself too hard, physically and mentally. Unable to sit at home in an empty house, he'd hired a limo and a driver to take him to work, staying there far longer than he should. And when he finally called his driver to take him back to the estate, he dreaded walking into a house that didn't have Tanna in it.

It had been two weeks and he was over feeling like crap. Dammit, he really envied the cavemen of the past. He wanted to go to London, wrap his hand around her hair and drag her back home.

No fuss, no talking… Yeah, those cavemen didn't realize how easy they had it.

That being said, even if forcing Tanna back to Boston had been an option, it wasn't something he'd ever do. He wanted her with him but more than that, he wanted her to *want* to be with him.

Nothing else would suffice.

So, long nights and busy days would be the way he'd be spending his time until he got the hell over her.

As if that was a possibility.

He was so sick of feeling…sick. Heartsore. Incapacitated. Slow. He wanted to walk freely, run, drive his damn car, make love without the discomfort of his cast. He wanted to go to sleep without having to take a pain pill or a sleeping pill or a combination of both, only to lie awake and ache for Tanna.

Man, he hurt. Physically and emotionally.

And, worst of all, he was starting to think she wasn't coming back. Not ever…

How the everlasting hell was he supposed to live the rest of his life without Tanna in it?

But he'd done it once; he'd have to suck it up and do it again.

His life…such fun.

"You look like hell, Brogan."

Levi closed his eyes at the sound of her voice and prayed, begged God, that he wasn't hallucinating, that she was standing in the doorway to his bathroom. Because if he opened his eyes and she wasn't there, he didn't know if he could stand it.

"Hey, Lee."

Levi opened his eyes and saw her reflection in the bathroom mirror, her hair pulled off her face, her eyes dominating her face. She looked pale and tired—someone else hadn't been sleeping much.

The fact that they both looked like ghouls gave him some hope. Levi released his grip on the basin and slowly turned around, allowing his good leg to take most of his weight. Yep, she was back, dressed in faded blue jeans, a red cashmere sweater and her favorite black coat.

Swear to God, he was going to strip her naked and kidnap her clothes. She was never leaving him again.

He didn't give a crap. He was letting his inner caveman loose...

"How's the leg? And your shoulder?"

Like that was important. Levi finally managed to get his tongue to form words. "Come here," he growled.

Tanna tipped her head to the side, as if she was debating whether to obey him or not, but then she started to move. When he could reach her, he placed both his hands on her hips and yanked her into him, his mouth covering hers. God, he needed this; he needed her.

In his arms, melded to him, just like this...

Levi pushed his hands into her thick hair, keeping her head still as he devoured her mouth, reacquainted himself with her taste. There was a hint of coffee on her tongue but mostly he could taste her... Tanna. His head swam.

She was here and he wasn't letting her go. Not again. He didn't care if he had to beg or grovel or move to bloody London, he was going to live his life with her.

She was his person...the other half of his soul.

Cool feminine hands skimmed down his rib cage and long, elegant fingers fluttered over his stomach and slid over the skin just above his towel. His body was telling her how happy it was to see her again and Tanna's thumb drifted over his erection. Levi groaned.

This would be a good time to sweep her into his arms, carry her up the stairs and toss her on the bed. He wanted to do that, more than he wanted to breathe. "I wish I could carry you to bed."

"In a few weeks, I'll hold you to your wish." Tanna murmured her reply against his mouth. "But for now, let me love you."

The towel fell to the floor and Tanna's hands wrapped around his shaft, setting off red and blue and gold fireworks in his brain.

Wait…what did that mean?

Was she back to stay or was she just going to stay until he was fully recovered?

Levi started to ask her but then she dropped to her knees, covered him with her lips and Levi forgot how to talk. Or think.

He could only grip the basin behind him as waves of pleasure rolled over him.

A little while later, Tanna pushed a cup of coffee across the kitchen table toward Levi, who was still looking at her with a what-the-hell-is-happening expression on his bemused face. Tanna lifted her mug to her lips to hide her smile. She hadn't planned on making love to her man in that particular way as a honey-I'm-home gift, but it was hella effective.

And she rather liked seeing Levi caught off guard.

Levi, now dressed in track pants and a Henley, sleeves pushed above his elbows, looked at her as if deciding whether she was a figment of his imagination or not. To help him along, Tanna pinched the skin on the top of his hand.

"Ow!" Levi glared at her. "What the hell?"

"I'm back—get used to it," Tanna told him, taking the seat opposite.

Levi carefully placed his coffee cup on the table and pushed it away from himself. He rested his forearms on the table too, and sent Tanna a hard look. "As happy as I am to see you, and as much as I enjoyed what happened in the bathroom, I'm going to be brutally honest with you, Tan."

"What? Just for a change?"

Levi ignored her sarcastic quip. "If you're not staying or if you intend to leave again in a few weeks, just do it now. Just walk out and don't come back. I want you, God knows how much I want you, but I can't handle you jumping in and out of my life, Tanna." Levi pushed a shaking hand through his hair and Tanna's throat closed at the emotion in his eyes. "I love you, dammit, but I'm an all-or-nothing type of guy."

"I know, Lee."

Tanna held his eyes, but didn't say anything more. She wanted to tell him she'd packed up her apartment in London, that all her furniture, books and boxes were in a container and were due to arrive in Boston in a week. She wanted to ask him whether she should rent an apartment or move back into the house in Beacon Hill or whether he wanted her here. Whether he'd consider marriage again, children...

With her obviously. But the words, big and hot and scary, were stuck in her throat. Why couldn't she say anything? Why now, at one of the most important times of her life, was her brain overloading, her tongue not functional?

Because this was so big, so important, so life-changing...

And she was terrified.

Levi pushed his chair back and started to stand up. "Okay, well, your silence is your answer."

Wait! What? No, it wasn't!

Tanna leaned forward and cleared her throat. "Sit down, Levi. Please?"

Levi glared at her, obviously frustrated, but he sat down, his eyes on his mug of coffee. Tanna, knowing it was do-or-die time, cleared her throat. She didn't have time to marshal her thoughts or pick her words, she just had to speak. "I'm a lucky woman, Lee. So incredibly blessed."

Levi narrowed his eyes at her, frustration leaping into them. "Are you really going to spout that BS again?"

Tanna smiled at his irritation. "I *am* lucky, Levi. I had a couple of bad things happen to me but really, in the scheme of things, I was extremely fortunate. I had my brothers when my parents died, I had excellent medical care and I found you. Being loved by you has been the greatest blessing of my life."

"But?"

Tanna reached across the table and placed her hand on his wrist, tracing the raised veins with the tips of her finger. "I'm sorry for the way I left you, Levi, but I'm not sorry for leaving. I needed to do that. I needed to live a different life. I needed to do what I did. I very much needed to stand on my own two feet."

"You're not telling me anything new here, Murphy," Levi growled, impatient.

Tanna stroked the length of his ring finger. "But

I'm done with feeling guilty, done with thinking I don't deserve love and happiness because I lived this sprinkled-with-fairy-dust life."

"You lost your parents, you had an accident and you worked your ass off to walk again. Where was the fairy dust while you were in the hospital?" Levi demanded.

"You were my fairy dust, Lee. You and your mom and my brothers, you were there every step of the way. In the midst of my pain, I fell in love—who does that happen to?—and I got a mom at the same time. I fell in love with Callie about the same time I fell in love with you."

Tanna touched her top lip with her tongue. "Back then, and up until recently, I couldn't help contrasting my life with Addy's. I felt guilty and the guilt grew and grew. I needed time to work through it, to work through a bunch of stuff."

"Are you done with that?" Levi asked her, his tone gruff but his eyes, finally, hopeful.

Tanna nodded. "Yep, I'm done. I mean, I feel incredibly lucky but I'm going to just be grateful and not let my past stop me from being happy. From living the life I want to lead."

Levi tangled his fingers in hers, his grip tight. "And what type of life do you want to lead, Murphy?"

Tanna shrugged. "It doesn't matter, as long as you're in it. I'll take anything you can give me." Tears brightened her eyes. "I'm not proud. I just want you, however I can get you."

Levi stared at her for a long minute, maybe two, and Tanna squirmed in her chair, wishing she could figure out what was going on in those dark blue eyes. His were the eyes she wanted to look into for the rest of her life.

"Nope. I'm not buying that. What do you really want?" Levi demanded. "I need to know, Tanna."

Okay, laying her heart on the line here. Fine, she could do this. She *would* do this. This was only the rest of her life she was fighting for. She'd start with the easy stuff.

"I spoke to Carrick earlier and he wants me to join Murphy's, help out in PR, be the liaison for their wealthiest clients."

Levi narrowed his eyes. "Is working for Murphy's absolutely what you want to do? What about being an EMT? You worked hard to qualify, and it's important too."

His concern over her happiness made her feel all squishy inside. "I'm going to find an organization that can use my skills on a part-time, volunteer basis. Professionally, I think it's a balance that will work for me."

Levi nodded and Tanna saw his agreement in his eyes. Right, now came the hard part...

"Personally, I want to be able to tell the movers to deliver my furniture to this house. I want to move my clothes into a closet next to yours, use your shoulder as a pillow. I want to wake up every day to the sound of your breathing. I want to see your smile, feel your mouth on my skin, make love as often as we possibly can." Tanna broke off, conscious she was babbling.

Levi gestured for her to continue.

"I want to give you babies, fight with you, laugh with you." Tanna looked for a last little bit of courage.

"I want the wedding we never had. But wedding or not, I really, really, want to be your wife."

Levi's eyes lightened and hope flared when she saw the humor in his eyes. He shrugged, aiming for casual when she knew he was feeling anything but. "So… ask me."

Tanna frowned, puzzled. "What?"

"I asked the last time. It's your turn now," Levi told her, leaning back in his chair, a small smile on his face.

His meaning sank in. Seriously? He wanted her to do this?

Levi made a circular motion with his index finger. "I'm growing old here, Murphy."

Laughing, Tanna placed both her hands on his forearms and dug her fingers into his bare skin. "Will you marry me, Levi Brogan?"

If he said no, after all this, she'd slap him. Really, really hard.

"And why do you want to marry me, Tan?"

Hadn't she explained all that in her rambling speech earlier? Then Tanna realized what she'd left out and she swallowed, tears clogging her throat. "Because I love you, Lee. So very much."

"Thank God." Levi leaned across the table and touched her lips in the sweetest, sexiest kiss she'd ever experienced. He pulled back, touched her cheek and smiled. "Are you going to bail on me again, Murphy?"

"I promise you I won't. If you say yes, I'm in this for the whole for better and for worse, richer, poorer, death do us part deal."

Levi grinned. "No obey?"

"Nice try, Lee." Tanna rose, walked around the table and plopped herself on his lap. Levi's arms immediately went around her waist to hold her tight, his mouth on her temple. After exchanging tender kisses, Tanna pulled back and stroked his cheek with her thumb. "You didn't give me an answer, Lee."

"You know my answer, baby." Levi placed his hand on her heart and copped a feel while he was at it. "Yes. To everything. To moving in, to babies, to marriage…"

Levi cuddled her close and Tanna felt like her life was starting over, as if she was cracking open a brand-new journal, the white pages begging her to fill the pages with love and beauty.

"I also say yes to spontaneous sex in the bathroom."

And laughter, Tanna thought as she blushed. They'd fill their lives, and the journal, with love and happiness, great sex and a whole bunch of laughter.

It sounded perfect, and best of all, she finally felt like she deserved this very wonderful man, and the life she'd been given a second chance at having.

She wouldn't, she vowed, waste a second of it.

* * * * *

Look for the Murphy brothers' stories,
coming soon!
Carrick's story will be available
February 2020!
Only from Joss Wood and Harlequin Desire!

Get 4 FREE REWARDS!

We'll send you 2 FREE Books
plus 2 FREE Mystery Gifts.

Harlequin® Desire books feature heroes who have it all: wealth, status, incredible good looks... everything but the right woman.

FREE
Value Over
$20

SPECIAL EXCERPT FROM

A flash of pink moving around in his house made Kaegan frown when he
recalled just who'd worn that particular color tonight. He glanced back at
Sasha. "Tell Farley that I hope he starts feeling better. Good night." Without
waiting for Sasha's response, he quickly walked off, heading inside his
home.

He heard a noise coming from the kitchen. Moving quickly, he walked
in to find Bryce Witherspoon on a ladder putting something in one of the
cabinets. Anger, to a degree he hadn't felt in a long time, consumed him.
Standing there in his kitchen on that ladder was the one and only woman
he'd ever loved. The one woman he would risk his life for, and he recalled
doing so once. She was the only woman who'd had his heart from the time
they were in grade school. The only one he'd ever wanted to marry, have his
babies. The only one who...

He realized he'd been standing there recalling things he preferred not
remembering. What he should be remembering was that she was the woman
who'd broken his heart. "What the hell are you doing in here, Bryce?"

His loud, booming voice startled her. She jerked around, lost her balance
and came tumbling off the ladder. He rushed over and caught her in his arms
before she could hit the floor. His chest tightened and his nerves, and a few
other parts of his anatomy, kicked in the moment his hands and arms touched
the body he used to know as well as his own. A body he'd introduced to
passion. A body he'd—

"Put me down, Kaegan Chambray!"

He started to drop her, just for the hell of it. She was such a damn ingrate.
"Next time I'll just let you fall on your ass," he snapped, placing her on her
feet and trying not to notice how beautiful she was. Her eyes were a cross
of hazel and moss green, and were adorned by long eyelashes. She had high
cheekbones and shoulder-length curly brown hair. Her skin was a gorgeous
honey brown and her lips, although at the moment curved in a frown, had
always been one of her most noticeable traits.

"Let go of my hand, Kaegan!"

Her sharp tone made him realize he'd been standing there staring at her. He fought to regain his senses. "What are you doing, going through my cabinets?"

She rounded on him, tossing all that beautiful hair out of her face. "I was on that ladder putting your spices back in the cabinets."

He crossed his arms over his chest. "Why?"

"Because I was helping you tidy up after the party by putting things away."

She had to be kidding. "I don't need your help."

"Fine! I'll leave, then. You can take Vashti home."

Take Vashti home? What the hell was she talking about? He was about to ask when Vashti burst into the kitchen. "What in the world is going on? I heard the two of you yelling and screaming all the way in the bathroom."

Kaegan turned to Vashti. "What is she talking about, me taking you home? Where's Sawyer?"

"He got a call and had to leave. I asked Bryce to drop me off at home. I also asked her to assist me in helping you straighten up before we left."

"I don't need help."

Bryce rounded on him. "Why don't you tell her what you told me? Namely, that you don't need *my* help."

He had no problem doing that. Glancing back at Vashti, he said. "I don't need Bryce's help. Nor do I want it."

Bryce looked at Vashti. "I'm leaving. You either come with me now or he can take you home."

Vashti looked from one to the other and then threw up her hands in frustration. "I'm leaving with you, Bryce. I'll be out to the car in a minute."

When Bryce walked out of the kitchen, Kaegan turned to Vashti. "You had no right asking her to stay here after the party to do anything, Vashti. I don't want her here. The only reason I even invited her is because of you."

Kaegan had seen fire in Vashti's eyes before, but it had never been directed at him. Now it was. She crossed the room and he had a mind to take a step back, but he didn't. "I'm sick and tired of you acting like an ass where Bryce is concerned, Kaegan. When will you wake up and realize what you accused her of all those years ago is not true?"

He glared at her. "Oh? Is that what she told you? News flash—you weren't there, Vashti, and I know what I saw."

"Do you?"

"Yes. So, you can believe the lie she's telling you all you want, but I know what I saw that night."

Vashti drew in a deep breath. "Do you? Or do you only know what you think you saw?"

Then without saying anything else, she turned and walked out of the kitchen.

SPECIAL EXCERPT FROM

HARLEQUIN® *Desire*

*Becoming guardian of his young niece is tough
for Westmoreland neighbor Pete Higgins.
But Myra Hollister, the irresistible new nanny with a
dangerous past, pushes him to the brink. Will desire for
the nanny distract him from duty to his niece?*

Read on for a sneak peek at
Duty or Desire
by New York Times *bestselling author Brenda Jackson!*

"That's it, Peterson Higgins, no more. You've had three servings already," Myra said, laughing, as she guarded the pan of peach cobbler on the counter.

He stood in front of her, grinning from ear to ear. "You should not have baked it so well. It was delicious."

"Thanks, but flattery won't get you any more peach cobbler tonight. You've had your limit."

He crossed his arms over his chest. "I could have you arrested, you know."

Crossing her arms over her own chest, she tilted her chin and couldn't stop grinning. "On what charge?"

The charge that immediately came to Pete's mind was that she was so darn beautiful. Irresistible. But he figured that was something he could not say.

She snapped her fingers in front of his face to reclaim his attention. "If you have to think that hard about a charge, then that means there isn't one."

"Oh, you'll be surprised what all I can do, Myra."

She tilted her head to the side as if to look at him better. "Do tell, Pete."

Her words—those three little words—made a full-blown attack on his senses. He drew in a shaky breath, then touched her chin. She blinked, as if startled by his touch. "How about 'do show,' Myra?"

Pete watched the way the lump formed in her throat and detected her shift in breathing. He could even hear the pounding of her heart. Damn, she smelled good, and she looked good, too. Always did.

"I'm not sure what 'do show' means," she said in a voice that was as shaky as his had been.

He tilted her chin up to gaze into her eyes, as well as to study the shape of her exquisite lips. "Then let me demonstrate, Ms. Hollister," he said, lowering his mouth to hers.

The moment he swept his tongue inside her mouth and tasted her, he was a goner. It took every ounce of strength he had to keep the kiss gentle when he wanted to devour her mouth with a hunger he felt all the way in his bones. A part of him wanted to take the kiss deeper, but then another part wanted to savor her taste. Honestly, either worked for him as long as she felt the passion between them.

He had wanted her from the moment he'd set eyes on her, but he'd fought the desire. He could no longer do that. He was a man known to forego his own needs and desires, but tonight he couldn't.

Whispering close to her ear, he said, "Peach cobbler isn't the only thing I could become addicted to, Myra."

Will their first kiss distract him from his duty?

Find out in
Duty or Desire
by New York Times *bestselling author Brenda Jackson.*

Available December 2019 wherever
Harlequin® Desire books and ebooks are sold.

Harlequin.com